I0619538

SLEUTHING IN THE PINK

A PARANORMAL COZY MYSTERY

A WITCH'S COVE MYSTERY
BOOK FOUR

VELLA DAY

EROTIC READS PUBLISHING

ABOUT THE BOOK

A new job. A new hobby. And then death by bowling pin.

Hi, I'm Glinda Goodall. After enjoying my waitressing job at my aunt's restaurant for the last three years, I got sucked into opening up my own private investigation firm—as an amateur sleuth, of course. Just because I was a good listener [read: gossip seeker] and helped solve a few crimes, that didn't mean I had any business hanging up my shingle. But hang it I did.

In need of a different gossip source, my partner and I joined a bowling league. I know, right? I've shunned anything to do with athletics my whole life. Just my luck, the league had only begun when someone ends up dead on the alley with a pin in his mouth—make that a pink pin. And no, I didn't kill him, not that everyone believes me.

But don't worry. I'll be fine. I just needed to find the killer. If you need to find me, I'll either be working part time at the

Tiki Hut Grill or at my new digs above the Wine and Cheese Emporium.

CHAPTER 1

"What do you think?" I held up the wooden sign that my new partner in crime, Jaxson Harrison, promised he'd mount outside our new office tomorrow.

Penny Carsted, one of my best friends and fellow coworkers, raised her wine glass in a toast. "It's amazing. To Glinda Goodall and The Pink Iguana Sleuths!"

I leaned the wooden plaque against my sofa, grabbed my glass, and touched my drink to hers. "To The Pink Iguana Sleuths." I inhaled the joy, only to let reality seep in. I sighed.

"Is something wrong?" Penny asked.

Darn. I hadn't wanted to share my insecurities with her tonight, because she seemed so happy, but what were friends for?

"What if I'm making a mistake by starting my own firm— and with Jaxson, no less?" I slipped next to her on the sofa. "I'll miss talking and sharing things with you if we aren't working side by side every day."

"It's not like we can't visit."

"True, and it's not like I won't be working here for the

near foreseeable future—at least until our business is up and running," I said.

"I agree, and starting your own firm is what the universe has always had in store for you. You're organized, focused, and determined to help others."

"I worry about expenses a bit, what with getting an office and setting it up." I don't know why I was whining. This was my dream.

"It won't cost you that much. Didn't you say that Drake isn't charging you any rent for the office space?"

Jaxson's younger brother, Drake, was my best male friend and owned the two-story building, the Howl at the Moon Wine and Cheese Emporium, just two buildings over from my second-floor apartment above the Tiki Hut Grill—make that my rent-free apartment. I did have the best aunt in the world.

"He is. I know it's perfect. Drake was using the second floor of his building as a storage room, but being a doll, he straightened it up for me—more or less." I don't know why I was worried. "The best part is that our new office has an outside staircase, a small bathroom, and even a tiny kitchen —one that currently is stacked with empty wine boxes." As I said, the place was more or less cleaned up. "I'm pretty sure he would have charged me if his brother wasn't part of the deal."

Penny lifted a shoulder. "That could be, but since Drake wants his brother to be happy, he'll do whatever it takes to make it happen. Besides, I think this new adventure will help both of you." She reached out and squeezed my hand.

"You're right."

Jaxson Harrison had come to town a few months ago after staying away from Witch's Cove for eleven years. Why that long? He'd been accused and convicted of a crime he hadn't committed. As a result, he'd served three years in jail for robbery. Thankfully, he was able to move forward with his life—kind of—by going back to school. Not only did he study some law, he'd earned a degree in computer science.

When he returned to test the waters, Witch's Cove was anything but friendly, thanks to the crooked sheriff and his deputy son. When the truth came out about Jaxson's innocence—partially thanks to yours truly—he was exonerated and his record was expunged. Ever since then Jaxson's outlook on life had improved greatly.

"I know I'm right," Penny said. "Now drink up."

I wanted to believe her more than anything. "Jaxson told me that he was feeling a bit restless working in Drake's back room, but I hope he isn't just joining forces with me because I helped clear his name."

"Nonsense. I haven't spoken to him recently, but from what you've told me, he seems to like working on cases."

"He does."

If anyone had told me a few months ago that I'd be partnering with Jaxson Harrison, I would have laughed in their faces. He wasn't my type when I was fifteen, and he was even less my type when he first returned home. He was angry. So angry. As long as he didn't take it out on clients, I could handle any mood swings.

After everyone learned that the sheriff had lied about Jaxson being the guilty party in the liquor store theft, his personality had totally transformed. It improved even more last week when the courts deemed Duncan Donut—or rather Sheriff William Duncan—guilty of lying on the stand. He received three years in jail, followed by three years' probation, and a three thousand dollar fine. It wouldn't give Jaxson his time back, but it did help his mental state.

"The truth is that I worry about going into business with him," I said.

"I don't see why?" Penny finished off her glass of wine. "Jaxson seems great. And he treats you well."

"He does. For now. But what if he becomes too controlling? Being protective is one thing, but if he insists we do things his way, it might be a problem."

If we ended up fighting all the time, it could be a deal breaker. It was why I promised myself to avoid arguing at all costs.

"He won't do that. He knows you're the witch."

"A witch with few powers. Every spell I've done of late seems to mess up things even more."

Penny set down her glass and wrapped an arm around my shoulder. "Stop obsessing."

"Obsession is my middle name."

She laughed. "That is what will make you a successful sleuth."

"You think?"

She smiled. "I know so."

"Thanks." It helped having the support. My aunt was on board with this new adventure, but my parents? Not so much. They'd been hounding me forever to find a real job that would use my math degree, but being a sleuth was too dangerous in their minds. Oh, well. I couldn't please everyone. It was what I wanted, so it was what I was going to do.

Penny sat back up and refilled her glass with the bottle I'd left on the coffee table. When the two of us got going, we could plow through one in no time.

"I really love the name of your new company—and the pink signage."

Penny was clearly trying to change the subject to cheer me up, and I appreciated that. I chuckled. "Well, it is the only color I wear."

"And I'm pink," Iggy said, lifting his chest. He'd been

sitting quietly—a rarity—on the edge of the coffee table for a while.

Iggy is my pink iguana familiar—make that my talking pink iguana. Anyone new to Witch's Cove probably would not know that when I was twelve, I went into the Hendrian Forest and conjured him up by doing a spell. Sure, I was hoping for a black cat—what pre-teen wouldn't wish for one—but I got Iggy instead. He claims he was born green, but when I came along, my obsession with wearing pink must have changed his color. Trust me, he hasn't let me forget it in the last fourteen years.

I will have to say that of late, he hasn't been complaining about it as much. It might be because I recently tried to do a spell to return him to his natural green state, but the spell went wrong—really wrong.

I inhaled to push aside my rather maudlin musings and smiled. I wanted Iggy to know how much I loved him. "Yes, everyone will flock to our company to ask for our help regarding their investigative needs, because I have the best pink iguana detective in Witch's Cove."

"I'm the only pink iguana in Witch's Cove or in all of Florida for that matter."

"True."

Poor Iggy. Ever since his new girlfriend refused to give him the time of day, he'd been a bit depressed. Then again, Aimee was a cat, so it was understandable.

"Is Jaxson okay with the firm's name?" Penny asked. "I thought he wanted Goodall and Harrison."

"He did at first, but the name wasn't exactly catchy. After we discussed it—and Iggy chimed in—Jaxson agreed with the new name mostly because he conceded that the firm is mine and that he is still merely the muscle."

"I love it," Penny said. "And he is all muscle. I have to say, it takes a secure man to work at a company with that name."

"Jaxson is very sure of himself."

"Do you know what I think about the sign?" Iggy asked, moving forward a bit, careful not to knock over the almost empty wine bottle.

I knew what he was going to say. "The best part is the pink iguana wearing the Sherlock Holmes' hat?" That and the name.

"Yup. And the magnifying glass implies I'm really smart."

I laughed. "You are smart, magnifying glass or not, but I thought it was a nice touch too. Putting your image on the sign was actually Jaxson's idea."

Having Jaxson Harrison as a partner—at least part time—was what convinced me to get into the amateur sleuth business in the first place. Would anyone actually pay us for our help? Only time would tell.

One thing for sure, if pursuing someone required me to carry a weapon, I'd have to turn the information over to Sheriff Rocker and let him handle it.

Our lawman was already aware that Iggy and I could communicate with one another, as well as the fact I am a witch with some abilities. It had taken some work to convince him that the occult was real, but now that he was a believer, it would make providing my sources much easier. I no longer had to worry that he'd dismiss me because I was some crazy waitress turned sleuth.

CHAPTER 2

Penny picked up her glass from the coffee table and leaned back. "This is nice," she said.

"What is?"

"Relaxing in your apartment while my mom watches Tommy." Tommy was Penny's seven-year-old. "I really needed this time away from it all."

"I couldn't agree more. We haven't had time to even chat."

These last few months had been hectic to say the least. First our deputy was murdered—and Penny's ex-husband had been accused of the crime. Then I drank a potion that some ancient witch had mixed wrong that enabled me to see ghosts. Let me tell you, that was a trip. While I could still see my dead uncle, I was thankful no one from the other side had contacted me recently.

"When are you officially opening?" Penny asked.

I blew out a breath. "That depends on when I finish setting up my office. I love Drake, but as I said, he's a packrat. To his credit, he installed a movable wall, so our clients won't see his junk."

She chuckled. "Who knew? His store is very organized."

"I know. It's like he has an evil twin who lives on the second floor—one who is messy."

Penny smiled. "I can so relate. I think I have an evil twin like that too. But putting up a wall to screen his belongings goes above and beyond."

"That's Drake for you. I just need to buy a few more pieces of furniture, and I'll be set. I really loved the comfortable vibe of Gertrude's office with her cushy sofas, the pink and white gingham curtains, and all the flowers." Gertrude Poole was Witch's Cove resident psychic and retired witch. She'd helped me many times to solve a case. "I have a black thumb when it comes to growing anything, so unless I go with plastic flowers, that design element isn't going to happen."

She laughed. "If you need help, let me know."

"I appreciate that, but my mother is insisting she lend her artistic talents."

Penny sat up. "Oh, no. Please don't tell me she wants to paint a rainbow on the wall."

I laughed. "I hope not. I was firm about not having any *Wizard of Oz* memorabilia in my office. I want my place to look professional. I don't think I could handle it if some client came into my office and suddenly burst into song singing, 'Somewhere Over the Rainbow'." Penny clasped a hand over her mouth, clearly trying not to laugh. "You've seen what she's done with the funeral home. Her yellow runner extends from the entrance to the viewing parlor. It's her tribute to the movie's brick road. That is way over-the-top, even for her," I said.

"I agree, but plants and fresh baked goods will really draw people in," Penny said.

I waved my glass at her. "I like your style." I snapped my fingers. "I forgot to ask, why aren't you out with your new beau, Hunter Ashwell, tonight?" Whenever her mom had agreed to babysit these last few weeks, Penny had gone out with him.

"He has a class to teach on how to hunt with a crossbow or something."

Hunter was a park ranger in the Hendrian Forest. "Interesting. Dad is at the funeral home, last I checked. He usually takes those classes, but he might have had a viewing or something and couldn't go. Did Hunter ever explain why he likes to hunt at night? I mean, don't you need to see the animal before you can shoot it?" I really needed to check on whether hunting at night was even legal. I probably hadn't looked because I didn't want to know the answer.

Penny smiled. "I think it's safer not to ask questions."

I had to give Penny credit. "I think you might be right."

They'd only been dating for a couple of weeks, but I'd never seen her happier. After all the stuff she'd gone through, she deserved a nice guy.

"How is Sam handling the new beau?" Since Penny hadn't complained about her ex-husband lately, I figured things were stable between them.

"He seems fine. I think he is actually seeing someone."

"Interesting, but you're not sure?" She shrugged. "Tommy hasn't mentioned her?"

"No. I figured Sam is being discrete."

Maybe her ex-husband had finally grown up. Good for him.

Penny polished off her wine. "I have to work tomorrow, but this has been great. I am so proud of you for realizing your dreams." She leaned over and hugged me.

"Thanks. Let's hope I'm just as excited about this in a month."

"You will be."

Even though I no longer had to set my morning alarm to get up at five forty-five, my body was wide awake at six. Why? Why? Why?

I closed my eyes and ran through what I needed to do today. Jaxson said he'd hang the company sign and then help with the office setup. While he was there, I really needed to discuss some of our plans.

As much as I didn't want to get out of bed, I realized sleep was not going to happen for me this morning. I rose, washed and dressed, and then headed into the living room.

Iggy rotated his head and opened his eyes. "You're up early," he said.

"Don't remind me." Like a zombie, I shuffled into the kitchen, put on the pot of coffee, and fixed a plate of greens for him. His water bowl looked untouched from last night, so I left it for now.

"What's on the docket for today?" he asked in a too chipper voice.

Docket? He acted as if I was going to work for some judge. "More office work."

"I want to come with you."

I was wondering when he'd make that demand. I had promised him that he could be at the office if he behaved. I couldn't afford to have him scare the clients. I figured this could be a trial run, but if he chatted with me all day, he'd have to stay home. "Okay."

"Great. Do you have any specific office work in mind?"

"Are you applying for a position as a secretary or something?" It wasn't like he could answer the phone.

"That's not a bad idea!"

Iggy understood why that wouldn't work. Since I wanted

him to feel included in this start-up though, I told him what I hoped to accomplish. "I need to do a little cleaning and a bit of organizing. You?"

"I haven't figured it out yet, but we need to get the word out that we solve crimes—hard ones. We'll even take cold cases."

Was he angling to be my marketing expert? Interesting. I had to laugh though. "Cold cases? What shows have you been watching?" Did he even know what that meant?

"The same ones you watch. I don't know what's so funny. You're so focused on making money, you haven't been paying attention to the important stuff."

"Important stuff? To what are you referring, Master Sleuth?" This ought to be good.

"Getting clients and helping them. Their ability to pay should be of secondary concern."

He didn't believe that for one pink moment. That was the kind of thing I was always preaching. Iggy, on the other hand, just wanted fame, but now wasn't the time to have that debate.

"It's time to go," I announced after I gobbled down a bowl of cereal. "I have a long day scheduled."

I refused to think about my waitressing job. My Aunt Fern, who owned the Tiki Hut Grill, had hired an additional waitress since I would be cutting down on my hours. The girl wasn't very experienced, which meant Penny would have to train her. For that, I was sorry.

I put my dishes in the sink and then placed Iggy in my purse so he didn't have to walk the few hundred feet to the office. Drake had given me the key to the outside door, because he didn't open his shop until ten. There was an inside staircase situated in the back of his store, but my only option at the moment was to enter through the outside.

Once I opened up, I grunted. The place was still a mess,

and it smelled musty. Not only that, it was dark. Did I mention that I hate dark rooms? I was a light person. Sure, there was a window that overlooked the ocean, but I needed task lighting. I also needed some air circulation. Hopefully, I could convince Drake to let me install a fan. I also hoped that Jaxson was handy enough to put one up.

I opened my purse and let Iggy out. I then set up my laptop on my desk, ready to get to work. Most of the office furniture would be delivered in a few days, but I had the basics—a desk and two chairs. Once I bought some fabric, I'd ask Aunt Fern to make me some (yes, pink) curtains. I had to keep with the theme, of course.

For the next hour, I created a to-do list, while Iggy wandered around, apparently taking inventory.

"Hello?"

I jerked up my head and found Jaxson holding out a cup of my special blend of coffee from Miriam Daniel's Bubbling Cauldron Coffee Shop. The aroma was distinctive and very welcome. "You are my savior," I said as I grabbed hold of the delicious brew.

He grinned. "Does that mean my status has been elevated from Mr. Muscle to Mr. Savior?"

I laughed. I had said he was my muscle a long time ago. I guess he never forgot. Working with Jaxson would never be dull, that was for sure. "Could be."

He nodded to the computer. "Don't tell me we have a case already."

"Hardly. I can't spread the word about our new business until I have the sign." I glanced up at him as a hint for him to volunteer to install it, but then immediately grunted. "Oh, no. I forgot to bring it."

"No worries. Is it at your apartment?"

"Yes."

"Give me your keys, and I will take care of it."

"Thank you! You are the best."

He tapped a forefinger to his forehead in a mini salute. "Jaxson Harrison to the rescue…again. I'll be right back."

While he was so good-natured, I wondered how long that would last when I suggested our first order of business.

CHAPTER 3

Jaxson stepped into the office after taking only fifteen minutes to install The Pink Iguana Sleuths sign. "All done," he announced with pride.

"That was fast." Apparently, he was able to mount the sign with little difficulty. Not only was he strong, he was handy!

Trust me, if I tried to use an electric drill, there would be so many unwanted holes in the wall, it might harm the structural integrity of the whole building.

After placing the tools in his toolbox, he washed his hands in the bathroom sink, because the one in the kitchen was occupied with junk. "What's next?" he asked.

I only had one chair in front of my desk. "Have a seat."

His brows rose. "This sounds serious."

"Not really." I leaned forward. "If we're going to make this work, I'll need a network of friends who, shall we say, *know* things."

"You mean who are inclined to gossip." His chin tucked under. "But I thought you were tight with the five gossip queens of Witch's Cove. What more do you need?"

"I am in good with them, but I think we should expand

our horizon. Even if these ladies live for another thirty-years, they really only know things from the clientele who visit their establishments. Sure, Pearl comes in contact with all of the criminals, but I think we need another source." Pearl Dillsmith was Sheriff Rocker's grandmother and office receptionist. The woman was a font of information.

He huffed out a laugh. "You mean a younger demographic?"

That sounded harsh. "Or at least a different demographic."

"I'll bite. How are you planning to accomplish this?"

"We should join a bowling league." Don't worry, I really had given this a lot of thought.

He stared at me as if I had two heads. "Do you even know how to bowl?"

I should have been insulted, but I wasn't. "Everyone believes that I am a people person, spectating at events rather than participating, but as part of my physical education requirement in college, I took bowling."

"Were you any good?" he asked, his eyebrows raised.

"That's debatable. I used to score about a hundred on any given day, and I am happy to report, I didn't get many gutter balls."

A glint came to Jaxson's eye. "Is that because you are a witch?"

"What are you implying?"

"Could you say, do a little hand wave or recite a silent spell to guide the ball into that sweet spot between the head pin and the number three pin?"

I really didn't recall where any of the pins were located, but I was insulted that he'd think I would cheat. "I've never tried, nor would I."

His lips quirked into a cute little smirk. "But *could* you do it?" He held up a hand. "If we are going to be partners, I should learn what you are capable of. You know my talents—like researching people and installing signs. I should know your abilities."

He had a point. "Let's say telekinesis was never my strong point, but I can move some items a short distance." I looked at my apartment keys he'd placed on my desk. Concentrating on drawing them closer, I lowered my forefinger, extended my middle finger ever so subtly, and then touched my thumb to my forefinger.

I sucked in a breath. They moved! Albeit one inch.

Jaxson pumped a fist. "That's great. I'm impressed. Too bad the bowling alley is a bit longer than an inch."

I looked up at him. "Funny, funny. It's not something I practice. The tourists love to have their fortune told in Witch's Cove, have a Tarot card reading, or even ask to speak to a loved one—through a medium, of course—but I think they'd freak if they saw real magic."

"Like you being able to move objects with your mind?"

"Yes. I probably should practice more, but it takes less time just to pick up the dang thing. On the other hand, if I had any ability to teleport, I'd be working on that skill in a heartbeat."

He laughed. "Okay, cheating aside, tell me why you want to join a bowling league."

I went through the suggestions Aunt Fern had given me a while back regarding how to network. "I don't think joining a knitting club or a bridge club is really my thing—or yours for that matter."

Jaxson nodded. "Yeah, I'm not seeing knitting either. I don't wear wool. It itches."

I laughed. I so enjoyed his humor. "What about cards? Bridge isn't your thing either?"

"Bridge takes too much work. Now, poker, that is a man's game. "

I snapped my fingers and then grinned. "Are you pooh-poohing the idea of joining a bowling league because you don't want me to beat you?" Sure, a bowling score of one hundred wasn't a high bar, especially for someone as strong as Jaxson, but he might not know that if he'd never bowled.

He leaned back in his chair and stretched out his legs. "Oh, sweetheart. You couldn't beat me even if you cheated."

I grinned. "You're that confident?"

"I am."

"Then how about putting your money where your mouth is? We should do a little test run."

"I'm game. What shall we bet?"

"Loser buys lunch?"

"Deal, but not at the Tiki Hut. Your aunt would comp you the meal," he said.

He was too smart. "Fine."

I turned to Iggy. "Do you want to come? You'd have to stay in my purse if you do though."

"Is the grass green?"

I laughed. "Then hop in."

The bowling alley, aptly named Pinarama, was about two miles north of town. The parking lot was not as empty as I thought it would be, especially since it was an early weekday morning. However, school hadn't started yet, so I wouldn't be surprised to see some kids there.

As soon as I stepped inside the place, the crashing of pins, the smell of lane oil, or maybe it was perspiration, assaulted my nose. I was sure I'd get used to it eventually.

Iggy popped his head up from my bag and looked around. "I think I made a mistake in coming here."

I laughed. Jaxson looked over at me and then Iggy. "Was he complaining about something?"

I smiled. He knew my familiar well. "I'm guessing the noise and slight odor offends him."

"Slight odor?" Iggy said.

"Deal with it," I said to Iggy before I faced Jaxson. I didn't have time for his whining today. "Yes, I need to rent shoes."

Jaxson glanced over at the selection. "You might be out of luck."

"What are you talking about? I wear size seven, which is a very common size."

"True, but do you see any pink shoes?" he asked.

Darn. I hadn't thought this through. "I'll have to take one for the team, I guess."

"Let's do this."

After we rented shoes, I had to find a ball. My eye immediately spotted a dark rose-colored one. I didn't care how much it weighed. That was the one I would use.

When I tested it, however, it was quite light. From my one semester class, I'd learned that heavier balls had a tendency to knock down more pins—assuming one had control. I set down the pretty pink one and then tried a different ball—a black one. My fingers fit well in the holes, but in the end, I couldn't use it. It just wasn't the right color. I had to go back to the pink ball. Throughout my indecision, Jaxson had a grin on his face. I refused to ask him what that was about. I knew.

The Pinarama only had ten lanes, which didn't surprise me since this was Witch's Cove, after all. "What lane do we have?" I asked.

"Five. Come on."

Jaxson seemed to be enjoying this. The scoreboards were electronic, so writing down the wrong score wasn't possible. I liked that.

"I'll enter our names," I announced. I wanted him to go first so I could judge what I was up against.

"I saw what you did," he said. "But I get it. You're scared."

I cracked up. Jaxson was going down. But don't worry. I wouldn't cheat—even if I could.

As we were putting on our shoes from the cozy comfort of our lane, I checked out the other bowlers. Lane three consisted of five high school boys. I watched one boy throw the ball, and I had to say I was impressed. I wouldn't be surprised if they were on the high school bowling team.

Lane seven had a mom with two kids who couldn't have been more than ten or twelve, while lane eight had...I don't know what I would call him—an alien wannabe—or perhaps an alien hunter? He was wearing an aluminum foil cap that was homemade for sure. It was just bizarre. The fact he was by himself was sad though—unless he preferred it that way. "Psst. Jaxson."

He was about to step onto the lane, but he placed his ball in the return and came over. "What is it?"

I nodded to Tinfoil Head. "What do you think his deal is?"

"Does it matter?" He arched a brow.

His comment made me feel small. "No, but I'm curious about him. I'd love to know his story."

"Ask him."

I was friendly and nosy, but I wasn't the type to walk up to a stranger to find out why he was wearing a tinfoil hat. For once, I squelched my curiosity. "How about showing me what you got?" I needed to change the subject from my embarrassing comment.

"Sure thing."

Jaxson picked up his ball and stood a few feet back from the line. While I could only see his profile, it looked as if he was concentrating intensely. With a smooth three-step approach, he drew his arm back and released the ball with a lot of force. The ball looked as if he'd aimed too far to the right, but at the last moment it curled inward. Bam! He knocked down eight pins.

Even though we were competing for who bought lunch, I clapped. "Good job."

Jaxson spun around. "Thanks, but I haven't bowled in years."

"I haven't either. Just for the record, how good are you?"

"A man never tells his score."

I laughed. That was supposed to be a woman's comment when someone asked about her age. I'm twenty-six in case anyone wanted to know, and Jaxson was thirty-two.

His ball returned with a clunk. The teenagers to the left cheered. One of them had just made a strike, but Jaxson didn't seem to notice. The man had mad concentration skills.

Jaxson hefted the ball to his chest and then eased it onto the lane. It headed for both pins, but alas, he only knocked down one of them. Despite missing the spare, I was still impressed.

Even though I kind of enjoyed bowling, now that Jaxson would be watching, I was a little nervous. Letting him see my poor form would cause endless ribbing. But as I've said, I was here for the gossip, not the sport.

Without making any excuses about being rusty, I stepped up to the return and grabbed my ball. I'd been taught to focus on the little triangles close to the line. If I hit the third triangle to the right of the center, I would knock down something.

Since the ball was so light, I threw it with too much force and as a result had little control. Before the ball went ten feet, it was doomed. I didn't get a gutter ball, but I only knocked down four pins. When I turned around to wait for my ball to return, Jaxson was on his feet.

"If we don't want to look like total novices, can I give you some advice?"

Taking advice wasn't in my wheelhouse, but this was

Jaxson—my partner. Since he did seem to be quite good at this sport, I swallowed my pride. "Sure."

The ball returned. "Pick it up. I want to see how you're holding it."

After a long discussion on the proper way to hold the ball, the best approach, and how to aim, I was ready. The problem was that I couldn't keep all of his instructions in my head.

Just as I was about to test my newfound knowledge, a shout of excitement came from our right and distracted me. When I looked over—which I couldn't help myself from doing—Mr. Tinfoil Head's arms were extended in the air and all of the bowling pins had been knocked over. He'd made a strike. Nice.

"Give me a sec," Jaxson said. He walked up to the main area and stepped behind the man. Jaxson quickly returned. "Now that guy is the real deal."

"Because he got a strike?"

"No, because he made a Turkey."

I saw some kind of image flash on his screen. I had to search the recesses of my mind for what that meant. "Is that like three strikes in a row?"

"Yes. This guy is good—real good."

I huffed out a laugh. "Let's hope he's not in our bowling league."

"Ten bucks says he is."

Oh, boy. What had I talked myself into? Was it too late to join the knitting club?

CHAPTER 4

No surprise, I lost the game. Jaxson seemed to be proficient in everything he did. For the record, I scored a seventy-eight, which I considered almost a victory. It wasn't in the three digits but for not having bowled in many years, it wasn't bad. And Jaxson? He bowled a one hundred and forty. So much for being rusty. The man had a lot of potential.

"Who are we going to ask to be our third and fourth?" Jaxson asked as he chomped on his burger—a burger I would be paying for.

We were at the Spellbound Diner for our somewhat late lunch. "Drake and someone else maybe?" We forgot to ask if a team required two women.

"My brother isn't the bowling type. Plus, he works Thursday evenings."

Ugh. "Do you have any friends you could ask?"

He lowered his chin and then gulped down some of his Coke. "No. What about Penny and her new guy?"

"Hunter Ashwell? She has Tommy to take care of, but

maybe her mom could watch him. It would give those two more time to spend together."

We asked Carl, the manager at the front desk, when the league started, and much to our surprise, it began in two days! It was either sign up by tomorrow or wait another eight weeks until the next league began. For the sake of our business, that was unacceptable.

"It's not like we have a lot of time," Jaxson said.

"You're right. I'll ask her after she gets off work today." I checked my watch. I had an hour. "Are you sure you're okay with this?"

"Are you kidding? I had fun today. The chance to tease you is priceless."

"Make fun of me is more like it." Jaxson's comments had been cute and mostly constructive. "The league isn't cheap though. While I'm okay with paying for the two of us, I'm not sure if Penny can afford it."

During our league nights, we were to bowl three games. The shoe rental, the occasional drink, and any snacks would add up over the weeks.

"I say we pay for them," he said.

I did some mental math. "I think I can swing the cost, but I would let them know that they might have to do a little snooping for it."

Jaxson reached across the table and cupped my hand. "Glinda, stop worrying about money. I have plenty."

I laughed. His brother didn't pay him that well. "Did you rob your brother's till or something?" The second that came out of my mouth, my face heated. "I am so sorry. I wasn't accusing you of—"

He had gone to jail for supposedly robbing the local liquor store.

"Don't worry. I understood what you meant. Drake pays me

slightly above minimum wage, but I made a ton of money when I was programming at the tech firm. I was living at home at the time, so my expenses were nil. I was smart enough to know that finding a job as an ex-con might be difficult, so I saved up for a rainy day. Besides, I'll be working for Drake whenever I can."

I loved that he was willing to help, but this was my company. "I appreciate that. I will pay you back as soon as the firm is up and running."

"That's not necessary."

Yes, it was. After we finished lunch, Iggy and I headed to the Tiki Hut while Jaxson returned to his day job. He didn't like leaving his brother short-handed.

Since it was a few minutes to three, I took Iggy back to the apartment and then went downstairs to the restaurant to wait for Penny. She normally had Tuesdays off, but with the need to train the new girl, Penny had to change her schedule.

My friend grinned when she saw me. Since she was finishing up with a table, I refreshed the condiments, sugar packets, and salt and pepper shakers for her. She came over a few minutes later.

"Hey, how was your first day?" she asked.

"I have a lot to tell you. Do you have a minute to chat upstairs?"

"I should. I'll call mom and tell her I'll be a few minutes late." As soon as she spoke with her, we headed upstairs. "I can't wait to hear how it went."

After I poured us some tea, I went over my logic about needing a new source of gossipers. "Jax and I talked it over, and we decided we'd try a bowling league."

"Bowling, huh? Do you even bowl?"

Why did everyone assume I wasn't athletic. Okay, I really wasn't. "Sort of."

"Cool."

I explained how we bowled a game this afternoon. "I lost,

of course, and I had to buy him lunch, but I did have a lot of fun, despite not doing well."

"I'm happy for you."

"Thanks. Here's the problem." I explained about wanting to expand my circle of gossiping friends. "In order to have a team, we need two other members."

Penny stared at me. "Please don't say you want *me* to join you?" She laughed.

"We aren't there to win, just to chat with the other league players."

She shrugged. "If that's the case, I guess I could ask Hunter. He seems like the athletic type. I know he is super strong."

I mentally cheered. "That would be awesome. The first game is this Thursday." I held my breath, hoping she'd say her mom might be willing to commit for eight Thursdays.

"How much is it going to cost?"

I knew she'd ask. "For you and Hunter? Nothing. It's on the house—at least for the games and shoe rental. It will be a company deduction. Whether we will continue after one season, I don't know. It depends on what kind of gossipers they turn out to be."

Penny grinned. "This is so exciting. I get to be part of your company without having to do much."

I loved the way she looked at things. "Absolutely. Do you think you could ask Hunter? We need to sign up by tomorrow."

"Sure. He gets off work at six. I'll call him then. What time does the league start?"

"Seven."

"Perfect."

CHAPTER 5

I 'll be honest. I was nervous. And it wasn't because I was bowling where the score kind of mattered. It was that I had to wear a league shirt. And it was brown! Could they have picked a worse color? Okay, maybe orange. I was sick about it, but there was nothing I could do.

To help make me feel better, I scrounged up a pink scarf to wrap around my neck, though the shirt was still ugly. At least it didn't clash with my pink jeans.

The four of us were assigned to lane nine. One group was to our right and two teams were to our left. Wouldn't you know it, Tinfoil Head man was on lane seven. Not that I had any hopes of winning, but that sealed our loss.

The hardest thing we had to contend with was picking a name for our team. The other three teams were in order from right to left: Pocket Pounders, Livin' On a Spare, and The Bowling Stones.

Ours? We went with The Pin-K Chasers. I thought it was cute, but it was creative Penny who came up with the name.

Jaxson was up first, then me, followed by Penny and then Hunter. I couldn't get a good sense about him, other than he seemed to like Penny. I could tell from his comments though, that he'd rather be outside than in a loud bowling alley, and at the moment, I couldn't blame him. Being in the forest with the animals would be a lot more peaceful.

Logically, I was there to bowl, but my problem was that I wanted to watch everyone else to figure out the dynamics between the team members and then see whose brain I could pick.

Penny tapped me on the shoulder while Hunter was up. "Did you see everyone has nicknames but us?"

Nicknames? Maybe I'd bitten off more than I could chew. I glanced to the right. Sure enough, their team of four had Diving Dan, Lucky Lucy, Diamond Dirk, and Crafty Carol. I had no idea if they were couples, but I doubted it. No one seemed particularly interested in anyone.

To our left was Tinfoil Tim, who I guess was okay with the choice, Merry Mary, Hunky Hem, and Produce Polly. I was seeing a trend here. I couldn't see the names of the team two lanes over from us though.

I knew three of the four people on that fourth team. I bought my paperbacks from Betty and Frank Sanchez, and when I was flush with cash, I would have my nails professionally done at Priscilla DeLorean's Nail Spa.

Hunter finished his frame, and now it was Jaxson's turn.

"Jaxson, we need to have a little discussion," I said.

He came over. "What's up?" I explained about the nicknames. "I want us to fit in."

"Okay. Ah, how about putting me down for...ugh. What starts with the letter J?"

"Jaunty, jolly, jilted." No, that sounded bad. "I'm not the creative one. Penny?"

"Give me a sec. I'll come up with something."

"I got it," Jaxson said. "Jailhouse Jaxson."

I sucked in a breath. "That's a terrible idea. You've worked so hard to get rid of that stigma."

Jaxson placed a hand on my shoulder. "It's okay. It's just a game."

He was right. "If you're okay with that, then I'll be Gossipy Glinda."

Everyone laughed. A minute later, with everyone's input, we came up with Forest Fox for Hunter and Pretty Penny for my friend. When Hunter suggested it, she'd turned many shades of pink.

I changed the names in the machine, and we were off. I really wasn't into the bowling as much as I'd hoped. I was spending too much time checking out who I recognized from town. Hunky Hem, aka Ralph Hemsworth, ran the gym, located on Crystal Ball Avenue. Produce Polly worked at—you probably guessed it—the produce stand at the Fresh Market. As I said, I already knew Betty and Frank Sanchez as well as Priscilla DeLorean.

"You're up, Glinda," Hunter said.

Sheesh. I had to pay attention.

My frame was not spectacular, but I tried to remember what Jaxson had told me about following through and how to move my right leg out of the way when I swung. I was happy with knocking down eight pins.

When Penny stood at the line, she looked around, probably to make sure no one was paying attention to her. Since she was new at this, she didn't take an approach. Instead, she bent over and tossed the ball. It bounced. Then it headed straight to the gutter.

She swung around, her face a picture of disappointment. A second later, one of the men from the Pocket Pounders came over.

"Hey, little lady," he said, his gaze traveling from her face down to her feet.

Penny's brows furrowed. Even I was confused why he was there. "Yes?"

"I'm Diamond Dirk Draper." He held out his right hand, one that looked like he'd won a few Super Bowl rings. The diamonds glittered. I could guess where he got his name. "I've been bowling for many years. I give lessons if you ever need them." He handed her his card.

Really? That was a little tacky, especially if he'd watched Jaxson bowl. While Jax wouldn't be going on the pro tour anytime soon, he was more than capable of giving Penny some pointers.

"Ah, thanks," she said.

The rotund fifty-something year old man winked and then returned to the next lane. By now her ball had returned. It was time for some intervention. I stood up. "That was rude," I whispered.

"He meant well," Penny said.

The man glanced over at her and smiled. "I'd say he was interested in you for other reasons." I made sure to keep my voice low. I didn't need Hunter to go all he-man on us.

"Maybe, but don't worry. I have no intention of asking him. He's kind of creepy."

"Give the girl a break, Draper," Tinfoil Tim shouted from the next lane.

"Just trying to help. Go mind your own business," Diamond Dirk yelled back.

Okay, this was uncomfortable. Wanting to make it look like I was trying to help, I moved Penny over a half foot to the left. "Keep your eye on the center triangle." While aiming for the middle one wasn't the best suggestion, I wanted her to knock down a pin.

"I'll try. Thanks."

She picked up her ball and stood back from the line a whole foot. It was a start. With a small arc to her swing, she took aim. When she let go, the ball slowly made its way down the lane. Penny looked back over her shoulder. "I think this one will be good."

I loved that she was excited. When five pins fell over, she clapped. I was very happy for her. She trotted back, full of smiles.

Hunter and Jaxson bowled next. When it was my turn again, something really cool happened. A pink pin appeared as the head pin. "Do you guys see that?"

I must have squealed a little too loudly because Hunky Hem stepped over. "You're lucky."

"Why?"

"If you get a strike, the house will award you a prize. From what I've heard, it can be quite nice."

Thrills shot up my spine. "And if I don't?"

He shrugged. "I think you get something for a spare, but that's all. Just relax."

Relax? Not likely. "Thanks."

I looked over my shoulder to see if they had any suggestions. "You can do this, Glinda," Jaxson said.

Since I had nothing to lose, I inhaled and focused. I thought I delivered the ball flawlessly. When only seven pins fell, it was clear I hadn't. My attempt to knock down the rest failed. Oh, well.

By the time we began the third game, my arm was tired, and I was sure it would be sore tomorrow. I didn't exercise often, other than when I was waiting tables.

To make matters worse, my score kept getting lower as the night wore on, whereas everyone else's seemed to improve. The cheers from the other teams grew louder too— probably due to the amount of alcohol they were consuming —as did the comments between them. Most were in fun, but a few were a bit insulting.

I have to say, I was surprised when Tinfoil Tim shouted

over to Diamond Dirk and then pumped a fist after he made another Turkey. There definitely seemed to be a rivalry between those two.

When it was Hunter's turn, I took a short trip behind the other three teams to check out their scores. Pocket Pounders and Livin' On A Spare were neck and neck, with Pocket Pounders winning by a mere ten pins. As for the Bowling Stones, they did better than we did, but they were not in the same league as the other two.

When we finished the third game, I was ready to go. All in all, this had been a success. While I had made a few new friends, my body needed a break.

I had the feeling that Penny and Hunter enjoyed themselves too—and more than just because Hunter was a good bowler. Could that man throw a hard ball or what? I bet with practice he'd give Tinfoil Tim a run.

I patted myself on the back for suggesting this.

We were the first team to leave. I had the sense that the members of the other three teams would stay around and share some drinks. From what I had been able to glean from their conversations, they'd gone up against each other many times.

We said our goodbyes to Hunter and Penny in the parking lot and then headed home. Jaxson had driven. Since he lived on the other side of town, he dropped me off.

"I hope this works out; I had a good time," he said.

Worked out? What exactly did that mean? Or better yet, what did I want it to mean?

SINCE I HAD nothing scheduled today that required me to get up early, I decided to sleep in. The stars, however, were not aligned in my favor.

It took a moment to figure out that the noise that jarred me out of my slumber was coming from my front door. Say what?

From the insistent knocking, it was important. Not taking the time to change out of my pajamas, I threw on a pink flannel robe and my dark pink fluffy slippers and rushed to answer it. Talking to anyone before I'd had my coffee would not be pretty.

I looked through the peephole to make sure an alien hadn't come to abduct me—okay, I might have dreamed about Tinfoil Tim, trying to figure out what motivated him to wear a tinfoil hat. When I saw my visitor, my heart sank so fast, my knees almost buckled.

What was the sheriff doing at my door at whatever time it was in the morning? I yanked it open. "Sheriff?"

"I'm sorry to barge in so early, but it's important. May I come in?" His serious nature worried me.

I didn't think he'd take no for an answer. "Sure, but do you mind if I fix myself a cup of coffee? I don't think well without it."

"Of course." He followed me into the kitchen. It wasn't as if I had a door off my second-floor that would allow me to escape. Sheesh. Iggy remained on his stool, but he kept an eye on the newcomer.

"Can I offer you a cup?" I wanted to be friendly.

"No, thank you. Glinda, I have some bad news."

My hand shook so hard, I feared I'd drop the glass carafe I'd just picked up. I spun around. "What is it?"

"Dirk Draper was murdered last night."

Relief swamped me that is wasn't someone close to me. "Who?"

He pulled a list from his pocket. "He was in your bowling league."

The way he said bowling implied, he too, found it difficult to believe I would be participating in such a sport. My mind spun. "Do you mean Diamond Dirk?" Last names weren't listed on the overhead screens.

He ran a finger down the list. "Yes."

"He's dead?" I wanted to make sure I'd heard it right.

"He is. The maintenance man found him this morning on one of the lanes with a pink bowling pin in his mouth."

I pressed a palm to my face. That could have been the pink pin I tried to knock down. "I'm sorry, but I didn't really know him. The league only started last night."

I put the coffee in the coffee maker, filled the carafe with water, and then plugged it in. I leaned against the counter waiting for my drink to brew—and waited for my pulse to return to normal.

Steve sighed. "Glinda, I don't believe you have it in you to kill anyone, but you have to admit it looks a bit suspicious."

"Because the pin was pink?"

"In part."

He had to be kidding. "I realize it matches the branding of my new company, The Pink Iguana Sleuths, but I think the pink pin was used as a matter of convenience." To be honest, I think I was the only one who got the special pink pin all night. Someone would have had to go behind the lanes and find it, which might not have been easy.

"The Pink Iguana Sleuths?"

That was what he focused on? He acted as if he had no idea I had started a company. "Your grandmother didn't mention it to you?"

"No."

Now I was worried about Pearl. I explained that Jaxson and I had gone into business together. "Don't worry, we're planning on doing simple things like spying on cheating husbands, looking for stolen items, and things like that. I'll leave the murders to you and Nash."

"That's good to know."

However, since he now had basically accused me of the murder, I had a darn good reason to stick my nose into this investigation. "Are you questioning everyone on the teams?"

"We are."

That made me feel a little better. "There is a flaw to your thinking that someone might be trying to frame me since I like pink." It didn't matter that he hadn't specifically said anything about me being framed. He'd implied it.

"Indeed. What would that be?"

My coffee finished brewing, so I poured myself a cup. "Jaxson only installed our sign yesterday. We aren't open for business yet, so I bet no one knows I like pink."

He dipped his chin. "Most people on Witch's Cove know you like pink. If they didn't hear it from word of mouth, I imagine they have frequented the Tiki Hut Grill at one time or another."

I wagged a finger at him. "If that were the case, I'd have recognized more of the league members, and I barely knew anyone there—including the deceased."

"You might be right, but weren't you decked out in pink last night?"

For once in my life, I was happy I was wearing that ugly shirt. "No. Our bowling league shirts are brown. Not pink. And my shoes were red, white, and blue. I looked totally non-Glinda like. I bet even those I'd conversed with in the past didn't know it was me." I didn't see the need to mention that I wore a pink scarf and used a pink ball. I'd also worn my pink hair extensions, worn pink eyeliner, and painted my nails pink.

He handed me the paper he'd been holding. "Here is the list of the team members. How many do you really know?"

I stared at the list. "I know Frank and Betty Sanchez since I buy my books at their shop, Candles Bookstore. Ralph Hemsworth, who runs the gym, stops by the Tiki Hut on occasion. He was the one who told me what the pink pin stood for since one appeared on my lane when I was up." I scanned the rest of the names. "I kind of know Dan Sanders, since he owns the Dive Shop, but our paths don't cross often. Oh, and I do shop at the Fresh Market. I've seen Polly there on occasion. And Priscilla DeLorean sometimes does my nails. The rest I don't know." I hadn't realized there had been so many. I held up a hand. "That's not totally true. Two days ago, Jaxson and I went bowling and saw Tinfoil Tim, but we didn't speak."

"Tinfoil Tim?" He ran his gaze down his list. "You mean Tim Bowers?"

"I guess. He wore aluminum foil on his head. He's a bit strange but a great bowler."

"Aluminum foil?" He huffed out a laugh.

"Yeah, it's as if he believes aliens are going to steal his thoughts or something."

"I'll keep that in mind," Steve said, trying not to smile. He slipped the paper from my fingers. "Did Dirk get into a fight with anyone last night by any chance?"

I had to think about it. "I'd call it more of a warning than a fight." I explained that Penny was a really bad bowler. "Dirk came over to offer her some lessons. He even gave her his business card. Tinfoil Tim yelled something at Dirk about keeping away from her."

"I see. Thank you. As a precaution, Nash and I are asking everyone to remain in town until this is resolved."

A tight band squeezed my chest, taking away my ability to

breathe. "I really am a suspect?" I thought his questions were a formality.

"Everyone is a suspect."

I totally planned to do my own investigation then. I wasn't going to get stuck with a bum rap like Jaxson had eleven years ago.

Or had Steve come here wanting my help, but he didn't feel right asking? After all, I had helped with his last three cases. "Would you like me to talk to anyone for you? As in be your spy?"

"No. Glinda. Please, for once. Keep out of this."

Now I was offended. I wasn't about to tell him I wasn't capable of sitting idly by and doing nothing. Didn't the fact I was starting my own sleuthing firm imply I had to snoop? "Roger that."

He held up a finger. "Unless you hear that someone wanted Mr. Draper dead. Then let us know so Nash and I can investigate."

I saluted him.

As soon as Steve left, I needed to shower. I'd never been accused of a murder before, and I hoped the hot water would help clear the cobwebs from my brain and make sense of all of this. Before I did though, I needed to warn Jaxson to expect a visit from our men in blue—or in this case, our men in boring beige.

I called to tell him about my early morning visitor, but apparently Nash had already stopped by his house, making me wonder if either Steve or Nash ever slept.

"Did Nash say anything other than the guy had a pink bowling pin in his mouth?" I asked.

"No. He showed me the list of our other league members, but considering I was fairly new to town, he believed me when I said I didn't know anyone other than Penny and Hunter."

How nice it was that for once the cops didn't assume Jaxson was guilty because he was an ex-con—which he technically wasn't anyway.

My pulse soared. "Penny! I need to go downstairs and talk to her. I hope Steve or Nash don't question her in front of the customers. Not only would that be embarrassing for her, it might hurt Aunt Fern's business. The act of them being there her would make a few think she was guilty."

"Go do that. When the lanes open, I'll stop over at the bowling alley and ask the manager for another list of names. I can then do a background check on them if you want."

My heart warmed. "You rock. You knew I couldn't let this drop, didn't you?" Having a partner in crime soothed my soul.

He chuckled. "Of course, I knew. Have you drawn up your spreadsheet yet as to who might have wanted Dirk dead?"

He was teasing, but it was a good suggestion. "I will after breakfast. However, see what you can dig up on him. It might give us a clue as to who might have killed Dirk."

"What are you going to do?" he asked.

"I'm going to shower and then check on Penny. How about meeting me at the office as soon as you get the list from Pinarama?"

"Will do."

Jaxson was the best.

After washing up, I chatted with Aunt Fern while I waited for Penny to have a break

"I can't believe Pearl didn't call me. She's slipping," my aunt said.

"It's early, Aunt Fern. She might not even be at work yet."

"It doesn't matter. To accuse you is wrong on so many levels."

"He has to ask everyone." Even I understood that.

"Glinda!" Penny said with obvious joy.

"Excuse us, Aunt Fern."

I led Penny to the hallway across from the kitchen since I needed the privacy. I explained about Steve's unannounced visit and what he wanted.

"I was wondering why Steve was here."

"Did he talk to you?" I asked.

"No, I've been swamped."

"I bet he contacts you later," I said.

She shook her head. "I can't believe that Dirk guy is dead."

"Me, neither. Just so you know, I mentioned Diamond Dirk gave you his card with the offer to give you some lessons."

"That's okay. It doesn't mean I wanted to harm him."

"No. If anything, you'd want him alive so you could improve." I thought she'd be more scared that a fellow league member was killed, but apparently, she wasn't.

"Let the sheriff question me. I was with Hunter after we left the lanes. He'll vouch for my whereabouts."

That was interesting. "All night?"

Her face heated. "No. I have a son, you know."

"I do. Steve didn't say when Dirk died, which means he could have been killed any time after we left. We'll have to wait for the autopsy report to find out the details."

"Are you going to ask your mother to contact Dirk? Maybe he knows who murdered him," Penny said.

My mother could speak with the dead, but sometimes the message was lost in translation. "That's not a bad idea. Jaxson's going to see what he can dig up on this guy. I know nothing about him."

"Me neither." Someone called Penny's name. "Gotta go. Thanks for the heads up about our law enforcement visit."

"Sure."

Before I went to the office, I stopped across the street for two of Miriam's coffees to go. By now, Jaxson should have returned from Pinarama. I wanted to thank him for buying a cup for me the other day.

When I walked into the office, he was at my desk on the computer. He looked up and smiled. "Pull up a seat. I found something on our dearly deceased."

Already? The man was fast. I placed the coffee in front of him and moved the chair over so we were next to each other. "Do tell."

He inhaled. "That smells divine. Thanks." He took a sip and moaned his pleasure. "I called Pinarama instead of driving there. It saved me some time. I got the list of league members from the manager."

"That was easy. I thought he might not be willing to give it out."

Jaxson leaned back in his seat. "I told him I wanted to collect money for the funeral."

"That's very creative of you."

Jaxson smiled. "It gets even better. We got to chatting, and he told me that Dirk Draper and his third wife had moved to Witch's Cove about six months ago, from just south of Calgary, Canada."

"I had no idea he was a newcomer. That might limit his enemies. What did he do up there?"

"He sold tires. Apparently, he ran a big franchise. When he moved here, he got his real estate license. That's quite a change, if you ask me."

"The manager sure spilled his guts, didn't he?"

Jaxson smiled. "I can be persuasive when need be."

"Clearly. Anything else?"

"I've only begun to do a little digging, but if I believe his social media posts, the guy is loaded."

"He was pretty decked out in diamond rings, so that's probably where he got his nickname."

"My thoughts, exactly," Jaxson said.

Only then did I notice Jaxson was wearing a pink silicone wrist band. I tapped it. "Speaking of jewelry, this is new."

"I thought I should get with the program." He grinned.

"I like it." I nodded to the computer. I had the sense making a big deal of the band wasn't why Jaxson bought it. "Please continue."

"Mr. Draper does have a checkered past. His first wife took out a restraining order on him, and his second wife, with whom he had a child, claimed abuse."

That was interesting and yet horrifying at the same time. "Maybe he left Canada because he needed to get out of the country?" Since Jaxson was at my computer, I pulled open the desk drawer and withdrew a piece of paper and a pencil. "Do we know the current wife's name?"

"Sharon Draper. Housewife." Jaxson turned the computer to face me.

I whistled. "She's beautiful and many years younger than our larger-than-life dead man."

"For sure."

"Anything else?"

"Not yet, other than they live in Sedgewood Estates."

That was a ritzy part of town. "Any children with this woman?"

"Not that I've found," he said.

"That's good stuff. What about his team mates? Is there anything suspicious about them?"

He lowered his chin. "I haven't had time to delve into their pasts, but...I did learn that Lou Owens, one of his team-mates, wasn't there last night. He is married to Lucy Owens."

"Lucky Lucy?"

"Yes. She works for Diamond Dirk in his real estate office."

This was becoming intriguing, so I took notes. "I guess it would be nice to know how he died."

"I thought he had a pink bowling pin in his mouth?"

I sipped my now slightly cooled coffee. "Do you think that was what killed him though, or was the killer merely sending a message?"

Jaxson pushed back his chair and stretched out his legs. "I like the symbolic aspect, but I'm sure the medical examiner will be able to tell us more."

He didn't need to remind me that since my mother ran the funeral home, she and the good doctor often shared things. "If my mother knows anything about the death, she'll tell me."

"Great."

"You know, if his team was victorious—like they were last night—maybe someone was jealous of Dirk and his winning team."

"That would be good to know," he said. "I can give the Pinarama manager another call."

"That won't be necessary. I need a manicure."

He lifted my hand. "Your nails look good to me."

I laughed. "Priscilla DeLorean, a member of The Bowling Stones, owns the spa. I'm hoping she'll be willing to have a little chat. I'll make an appointment, hopefully for today."

"I can see why you wanted to expand your gossip tentacles."

I grinned. "I'm glad you recognize my genius."

He laughed. Okay, he was smart too.

CHAPTER 6

"I am totally devastated." Even though Priscilla DeLorean sniffled, I wasn't buying it. Because she was the spa's owner, I imagined she was programed not to speak ill of the dead. It wouldn't look good for business.

She pressed the cotton ball with the polish remover to my nail.

"My friends and I had only bowled that one time," I said. "I was impressed with Dirk's team. They looked really good."

Her lips pressed together. "They always won. After a while, it became annoying, but I think it motivated us to be better. Someday, we hope to win—not that we could. I mean, I'm bad. I tell myself it's my long nails that prevent me from having a good grip."

I wonder if I could use that excuse. "Who would you say was the second-best team?" I thought it obvious, but I needed her to keep talking.

She chuckled. "It wasn't my team, that's for sure. Tinfoil Tim is the best bowler by far, but his team doesn't always come through for him, despite Merry Mary and Hunky Hem having high handicaps."

I had jumped to the conclusion that Produce Polly would have needed one, but apparently, I was wrong. "Interesting. Mr. Hemsworth looks strong. I would have thought he'd be a high scorer."

"Oh, his is a beast, but Hunk throws the ball too hard. He doesn't understand that bowling is all about control. His attitude is a macho thing, I guess."

I was happy neither Jaxson nor Hunter felt the need to show how strong they were. Hunter wasn't built as well as Jaxson, but I think he was stronger—almost abnormally so. If he had better form, he could be one of the best bowlers around—assuming he liked the sport.

Priscilla finished taking off my polish and applied the base coat. I had chosen a fairly dark pink this time, a slight change from my usual pale pink. "What is the deal with Tim? Is he crazy enough to want to kill Dirk?" I thought I was doing a good job of asking questions without seeming to be too nosy.

"Tim, violent? Oh, no. At least I don't think so. He's a nut job for sure, but I can't see him harming anyone—other than an alien, of course." She smiled.

"Even over bowling? He seems to take the game seriously."

"I suppose, but he's too absorbed in his scientific world to worry about other humans."

Now my curiosity burned strong. "What does that mean?"

"Can't you guess? It's why he wears a tinfoil hat," she said. "Merry Mary told me that the windows in his house are covered in aluminum foil, too. Tim told her it was because he was abducted by aliens once, and he never wanted that to happen again."

I had to work not to laugh, but I shouldn't be one to talk. I never believed in ghosts until I saw one, and Morgan Oliver claimed his uncle was a werewolf, so maybe aliens did exist.

I'd have to see werewolves and aliens in person to believe in them, though.

"Poor guy. That is no way to live," I said.

"Not at all." She placed my freshly painted fingers in a nail dryer.

I casually mentioned a few other league members, but no one really stood out as a killer. "I heard that Dirk was a realtor. Do you think some competitor would want to do him in?"

"To be honest, I'm there to bowl—or so I tell myself—not to gossip, but I did hear that wife number three isn't all that thrilled with him."

That was juicy. So much for not being a gossip. "Why is that?"

"One of my nail techs did Sharon's nails last week, and she said that her husband had recently been gone a lot at night. He'd wander in at two in the morning. When she'd asked him about it, he said he was checking out some real estate, but we both know no one can see much at night." Priscilla leaned closer. "If you ask me, the man was having an affair."

"That sure sounds like it. If Sharon is his third wife, she had to suspect that might be the case."

"Totally."

That reminded me of my dad hunting at night. "I'd love to have Lucky Lucy's take on Diamond Dirk's death."

"I think she left right after you guys did, so I doubt she knows anything."

That was too bad. "Even if she didn't see anything, she might know if someone was out to get him."

Priscilla pulled my nails from the dryer and started with the final coat. "She's really friendly. Ask her."

I just might. After my nails were done, I returned to the office with an idea, one that Jaxson might not like. When I entered, he was still at my desk leaning over the computer. "The second desk should arrive tomorrow," I said.

He pushed back his chair. "Sorry. I'm on my laptop, but this was the only flat surface other than the counter in the wine room downstairs. Drake is making a mess with his baskets so I can't work there."

Only now did I see my laptop sat closed on the desk. "No problem. We can share." I inhaled. "Speaking of sharing, I'd like a favor."

He looked up. "Name it."

I explained what Priscilla told me. "That means I'd like to speak with Lucky Lucy Owens."

"Okay."

"She's a realtor."

The light in his eyes brightened. "Don't tell me you want to pretend to be a client?" The surprise in his voice wasn't welcome.

"Why not? She'll want to keep talking as long as we're interested in buying."

Jaxson laughed. "We?"

"She'll know a waitress can't afford a house, but the two of us might be able to. I'm not suggesting we look for a four-bedroom mansion, but she'd believe we'd buy a modest two-bedroom."

He smiled. "Only kidding you. Of course, I'm game. Of all the people in the league, Lucy would be the most likely person to know who Dirk had a beef with. She not only worked with him, she was on his bowling league. They probably shared a lot."

"That's what I was thinking."

He stood "No time like the present."

Jaxson drove us over to the real estate office, which was slightly north of downtown. It *was* possible Lucy wouldn't be working today because she was upset over the loss of a friend and colleague. On the other hand, she might be out with a client.

When Jaxson and I entered the office, I was pleased to find her at her desk. She looked up and smiled, but from the lack of recognition in her eyes, she didn't have any idea who I was. When her gaze shot to Jaxson, however, her mouth opened slightly. "I remember you," she said. "You are on that new bowling team."

The flirtatious voice sickened me. After all, she was a married woman.

"Yes," he said as he wrapped an arm around my waist and tugged. "In fact, Glinda and I are looking for a home, and we heard you're a realtor."

I would have stiffened had he been anyone else, but I couldn't deny snuggling against such a hunk was rather nice. I was also impressed that Jaxson thought so well on his feet.

"Have a seat and tell me what you're looking for."

He rattled off what seemed like my dream house. Too bad I'd never be able to afford something like that—even if I wanted to move, which I didn't. I lived above the restaurant. Not only didn't I have to commute to work, I had a killer view of the ocean. That kind of real estate would be impossible to match.

"Let me see what I have," she said scanning the listings on her MLS sheet.

I was not there to buy a house but rather to gossip. "I wanted to say I'm sorry about Dirk. I didn't know him very well, but he seemed like a great guy." That sounded lame, but when I was lying, my tone wasn't the sincerest.

Lucy looked up at me. "It is horrifying. I still haven't processed it. The Pocket Pounders have won every league tournament since Dirk moved here. He will be missed."

Not by everyone I bet. "Oh, really? I didn't know you guys hadn't been a team forever." Jaxson had learned that from the manager, but I didn't want Lucy to know we'd been investigating her teammate.

"He and Sharon moved here about six months ago from Canada. Since it snows there so much, he bowled. A lot."

"That makes sense. I always pictured Canadian men as hikers and hunters. Shows what I know. I feel sorry for his wife," I said, really meaning it. "I've seen first-hand what losing a spouse can do to a person." Like what happened to my Aunt Fern.

"I thought that too, but I called Sharon this morning. She's holding up well." Then Lucy leaned forward. "To be honest, I think she is relieved."

Okay, I didn't expect to hear that. "Relieved that he's dead?" I kept my voice soft in case there were other workers in the back.

"Let's say he had a wandering eye."

That was consistent with him not returning home until late at night. For a moment I wondered if Sharon might have done him in. After all he had a history of abuse. That was assuming the first two wives were being honest.

"I'm sorry to hear that." I wasn't sure what she expected me to say. I didn't know what else she could tell us, so it was time to escape. I was about to make up some reason to leave when I spotted a photo on her desk. "Is that your husband?"

She picked up the photo. "Yup. That's Lou. You didn't get to meet him since he wasn't feeling well yesterday."

Lou had dark brown hair and a scruffy beard. He probably wore one to cover up the fact his cheeks looked quite gaunt. "I hope he feels better."

"He'll be fine, thanks."

She didn't seem worried, and I didn't question her further. I wanted to ask her the usual questions about who might have wanted Diamond Dirk dead, but I had the sense

Lucy would have become a bit too suspicious if I did. "Do you have a restroom?" I asked.

I wanted to call Jaxson so that he could make up some excuse for why we needed to leave.

Lucy smiled again. "Of course. It's just down the hall."

I stood and made my way to the facilities. Once inside, I called him. I bet he was surprised to see my name on his screen.

"Jaxson Harrison."

I pumped a fist. I was glad he didn't say my name. "I'm calling to give you a work emergency. I think we've learned all we can."

"Sure, Bob, I'll be right over."

My partner was a smart man. I washed my hands and returned. Jaxson was standing, looking concerned. "Everything okay, hon?" I thought calling him *hon* was a good touch.

"I hate to do this, but I need to leave." He turned to Lucy. "We'll reschedule when work isn't so hectic."

"Of course." She handed us her card.

"Thank you."

Once in the car, I breathed a sigh of relief. "Ten bucks says we learned more about Diamond Dirk than either Steve or Nash did."

"There is something to be said about people's love of gossip."

"You can say that again."

During the short drive, we kept our thoughts to ourselves. I, for one, was trying to mentally list who my prime suspects might be, and I bet Jaxson was doing the same thing.

"How about a stop at the tea shop for a crueler?" Jaxson asked.

Someone raised him well. I still couldn't believe that

when I knew him all those years ago, he had been sullen and distant. Now, he was a new person.

"You don't have to twist my arm. I haven't eaten." Cereal didn't really count as a meal. Besides, it was almost time for lunch.

Once we were seated at Maude's Tea Shop and I ordered my usual specialty tea blend and a pastry, I leaned back. "Tell me your thoughts."

"On the suspects?" I nodded. "There are certainly a few of them. In no particular order, I'll start with Dirk's wife."

"I agree. If my husband stayed out until the wee hours of the morning and then told me he was looking at real estate, I'd think the man was cheating," I said.

"I'm betting Sharon was well aware that she was the third wife. She'd have to wonder why the first two marriages fell apart."

"I totally agree. Let's not forget, Dirk was well off. Maybe Sharon married him for his money, but then realized she couldn't put up with all of his secrecy."

Jaxson pointed a finger at me. "You are right. Sharon might have told her friends she thought he was cheating, but what if he had been involved in some illegal activity instead?"

"Like what? Selling fake diamond jewelry on the side?" I asked.

He shrugged. "It could be anything; this guy was no saint."

"That would imply there are others who could have done him in—like someone he was doing business on the side with."

"If that is the case, we might never figure it out. Not having access to fingerprints and bank records, we are at a disadvantage."

"True." I had my magic—when it worked—but I didn't see how that could help.

Maude came over and delivered our order. She set down

my ice tea and gave Jaxson his cup of coffee. "Thanks. Did you hear about the murder at Pinarama?" I asked, hoping she'd provide her usual gossip.

"I did. Pearl told me a few minutes ago. What a terrible way to die. Do you know anything about it?" From the eagerness in her eyes, she was dying for some gossip.

"Not much, other than he's dead. Steve is questioning all of the bowling league members, but he told me not to interfere."

Maude laughed. "Like that is going to stop you."

I liked this woman. "You are right. If you hear anything, and I mean anything about who might have wanted him dead, can you call me?"

I probably didn't need to give her my business card, but I was really proud of them. It made me feel so professional, so I handed her one.

"I love this. I know Fern is proud of you. And yes, I will contact you."

"Thanks."

As soon as Maude headed back to the counter, I faced Jaxson. "I agree that Sharon might be my number one suspect too. Who else?"

"We can't ignore Tinfoil Tim," he said.

"I don't want him to be guilty. He seems a little loony but nice."

Jaxson laughed. "You do realize that people say you are a little loony since you think you can talk to a pink iguana." He held up his hand. "I know you can, but others don't."

He had a point. "True. Tell me why you suspect our resident alien abductee?"

"If I were the best bowler and then some upstart arrived in town and joined a better team, I'd be a bit upset."

"Upset enough to kill him though?" I didn't see it.

"It's possible. I also suppose they could be connected on a

business level, and Diamond Dirk cheated him in some way." Jaxson sipped his coffee. "Who else do you suspect?"

"I really don't have any other suspects. I could make something up, but I am trying to find proof instead of relying solely on my gut feeling."

His smile was brief. "Sounds good. What's the next step?"

I had to think for a moment. "We should see if by any chance either of the two ex-wives have recently flown down to Florida. No one would know them here, and maybe one of them thought they could get away with doing him in."

"I love your imagination. I can check, but I'm not seeing it. If either of them were thinking of getting any insurance money, I imagine it would go to Sharon, his newest wife."

"You have a point, but perhaps their hatred festered to the point where they had to kill him. Or he might have been paying them alimony and then stopped. Just because he wore a lot of diamond rings doesn't mean he was flush with cash. He could have overspent what he got from selling his franchise and be in debt."

"I like the way you think," Jaxson said. "We should find out how he died. I don't even know if someone could die by having a bowling pin shoved down his throat unless he'd been incapacitated," Jaxson said. "Diamond Dirk was a large man, which is why I don't see a woman doing this."

"He might have been shot first or struck on the back of the head before that person shoved the pin in his mouth."

"This crime solving stuff is harder than I thought," Jaxson said.

"It is hard, but I have a good feeling about this. Someone will crack, and we'll find out who did this."

He smiled and lifted his coffee cup. "To the Pink Iguana Sleuths."

I tapped my glass to his, hoping I hadn't made a promise I couldn't keep.

CHAPTER 7

Once we finished our drinks, Jaxson and I went back to the office. It was time to regroup. He planned to research several of our suspects, while I did what I did best: I created a spreadsheet, listing the names, motives, means, and how sure I was that this person was guilty. It was anything but scientific, but without any evidence, it was the best I could do. I had to rely on hearsay. However, at the end of the day, I might present my case to the sheriff and let him run with it. It wasn't as if we were being paid for our time. Then again, there wasn't exactly a line outside our door waiting to hire us.

In the first column, I listed Sharon Draper, wife number three. She might have wanted her husband dead so she could get the life insurance money. If she had proof that he cheated on her, it might have given her more motive. The problem was I didn't see Mrs. Elegant going to the bowling alley and hitting him over the head with a bowling pin. Not only that, wouldn't her husband have seen that she was standing behind him? It made little sense. As much as I liked her for it, I had to give her only a fifty-percent chance of being the killer—unless she hired someone to carry out the deed.

Curious to know whether a bowling pin could actually knock someone out, I looked up to see how much it weighed. Pins came in various sizes between three and four pounds, which was not heavy enough in my mind to incapacitate someone for long, but I was no scientist.

Whoever the killer was, they'd have to have gone behind the lanes, grabbed that uniquely pink pin, worked their way to the front, moved up behind the deceased, and then swung the pin—assuming that was what killed him. The more I thought about it, the more I realized I needed to know the cause of death.

I pushed back my chair. "I'm going over to see my mother. I need to find out if she can learn what killed Diamond Dirk."

"The poor man hasn't been dead long enough for the doctor to have performed an autopsy."

"I know, but Dr. Sanchez should have an idea by looking at the body, wouldn't you think?"

"Could you get her to let you do your pink diamond crystal test on the man?" Jaxson asked.

"Not before she's had the chance to examine him," I said.

"And you think the medical examiner will tell your mom her thoughts before she does the autopsy? The sheriff, sure, but a friend?" he asked.

"I couldn't say for sure. My mom's job is to make the corpse's face look good in the coffin and knowing the cause of death can sometimes help her decide what to do."

Jaxson smiled. "Go. And good luck."

I headed next door and let myself in through the back exit. As usual, Mom was in her office. I went through the routine of petting Toto since he wouldn't stop barking until I greeted him properly.

"Oh, Glinda, I heard Mr. Draper died at the bowling alley. Weren't you there last night?"

"Did Aunt Fern tell you?"

"Yes, sweetie. She's worried about you. I can't believe the sheriff actually accused you."

Aunt Fern liked to embellish a story. "He didn't accuse me. He just wanted to know if I knew anything." Even if he had come out and said he thought I'd killed the man, I wouldn't have told Mom. She didn't need the worry.

"I'm glad."

"By any chance, did Dr. Sanchez mention how Mr. Draper died?"

"No. I often don't know. I mean, she might call to warn me if his face is marred, but that's all."

"The bowling pin in his mouth didn't do any damage?" I asked.

She sucked in a breath. "A bowling pin? How bizarre."

Apparently, she didn't know. "Have you tried to contact Mr. Draper?" I motioned upward with my eyes.

"Why should I?" She sucked in a breath. "Glinda Goodall, you are not thinking about trying to figure out who killed him, are you? You promised me you wouldn't do anything dangerous in your new company."

"I know what I said, but I couldn't handle it if the sheriff decides that since it was a *pink* bowling pin that maybe I was involved somehow."

"It was pink?"

"Yes, which makes me think someone might be framing me, though I couldn't imagine who."

My mother clapped for Toto who obediently raced over to her. She lifted him onto her lap. "This is highly disturbing."

"I know, right? That's why I need to look into things—under the radar."

She looked up at me. "The sheriff has no idea you're asking questions, does he?"

"No. Mind you, if I learn anything substantial, I'll certainly let him know."

She nodded. "I suppose I can give Elissa a call. I'll say I'd like to know if it will be an open or closed casket."

I breathed a sigh of relief. "Thank you."

"Don't thank me yet. Sometimes Dr. Sanchez is in a chatty mood, and other times, she'll tell me nothing."

"Thanks for at least trying." It wasn't like Steve Rocker would tell me. Unless it was obvious when he looked at the body, he might not know.

"I'll give her a call." Toto barked. "Can you take him for a *w-a-l-k* while I speak with Dr. Sanchez."

I figured she wanted to speak in private. "Sure. We'll take a stroll around the block."

I put on Toto's leash, grabbed a plastic bag just in case, and headed outside. The warm air was refreshing. Toto was a sniffer more than a walker. Making a small loop around the building took quite a long time. When I returned, Mom was not on the phone.

"Well?" I asked.

"She said Mr. Draper's death was caused by blunt force trauma to the back of the head."

"Wow. I can't believe a bowling pin could cause such damage."

"Oh, no, sweetie. It was a bowling ball, not a bowling pin."

That made sense. "Thank you for asking." I handed Toto, who was still on his leash, back to my mother.

I had to tell Jaxson. Even if I asked the weight of the ball, the medical examiner probably wouldn't know until she'd finished her autopsy. I just hoped the killer hadn't chosen my pink ball to kill Diamond Dirk.

"How is Dad doing?" It seemed as if his health would improve, and then he'd have a relapse.

My mother grinned. "It's a miracle."

I sat down. "Tell me."

"I don't know much, but ever since Stan started going into the woods, I swear his health has improved."

"Nature has a way of making things better."

"Not only better, but yesterday I saw him lift one end of a coffin as if it were a paperweight."

That was an exaggeration no doubt, but it was still impressive. "That's hard to believe."

"I know. He's sharper and more alive than ever."

"I'm thrilled." I didn't know what else to say. My father was a very laid-back man, and I couldn't imagine him taking drugs to bring about this new vitality. "Is he here?"

"He's with a family."

"I see." I stood. "I need to tell Jaxson what the medical examiner found out."

"Please say hi for me."

"I will." On my way back to the office, my mind spun. Hefting even a ten-pound ball would take some strength, let alone swing it with any momentum. Jaxson might be right. We should narrow down the suspects to men.

I walked into the office to find two men delivering our office furniture with Jaxson directing traffic. Excitement raced through me. We had discussed the location of everything, so I let him do his magic with the men.

In no time, I had a real office, complete with a love seat and two comfy chairs around a wooden coffee table. Jaxson wanted glass, but when I asked if he'd be the one to clean it every day, he said no. So, wood it was.

"I love it," I said.

"It does look great."

"I have news," I announced as I sat behind my desk after the delivery men left.

Jaxson leaned a hip on the edge. "What did your mom find out?"

"That Diamond Dirk was killed with a bowling ball—hit to the back of his head."

He whistled. "That changes things."

"I know."

"I think we should talk to the Pinarama manager again. He has to have noticed who the last people were to leave."

"Worse case, he says he doesn't remember. Or he lies."

"If Penny weren't working, I'd ask her to come."

He chuckled. "The human lie detector?" I nodded. "I heard she didn't do so well the last time."

That would be the case that involved the former deputy's death. "No."

I pushed back my chair. "Let's see what Carl has to say."

Jaxson drove. When we entered the bowling alley, a young man was manning the desk. Darn. Jaxson stood tall, probably just to tower over the kid. "Is Carl here?" Jaxson asked as he slipped our Pink Iguana Sleuths business card across the desktop.

I doubted it would carry any weight, but it was worth a try.

"You're private investigators," he announced with respect. I didn't see the need to correct him. "I'll tell Carl you want to speak with him."

As soon as the young boy disappeared, I held up a palm and smiled. Jaxson gave me a high five. A second later, the boy returned with Carl in tow.

"Oh, it's you," he said to Jaxson. "How can I help you?"

"Can we speak someplace quieter?" I asked.

"Sure." He pointed to the door we'd passed when we

entered the building. Carl slipped into his office and opened it.

We stepped inside. Since I didn't want Jaxson to have to lie, I spoke up. "Not that I don't think the sheriff and his brand-new deputy aren't capable of solving Mr. Draper's murder, but I'm not sure it's a priority for them."

My face heated from the lie, but I felt we had a good chance of finding the culprit. If I had to resort to a little magic to do it, I wasn't against it.

"How can I help? I told the sheriff everything."

"Can you go over it again?" Jaxson asked. "Sometimes you remember something the second time."

Carl shrugged. "Sure. Many times after the league ends, and everyone is gone, I'll challenge Dirk to a game." He pointed to a wall of plaques. "I used to be good, but with my arthritic knee, the best I can do is play a few games a week."

"I'm sorry." I couldn't imagine not being able to do what you loved. "Did you bowl a game last night?"

"I did. Dirk won, as usual, but I was pleased with my score. After that, we shook hands, and I went back into my office to tally up the day's receipts."

"Did Dirk leave?" I asked.

"No. He wanted to get in a few more frames. I was fine with that. I must have worked another half hour. The noise had stopped, so I assumed Dirk had gone. I exited by the door you two came in. Since we had played on lane ten, even if I had looked in that direction, I wouldn't have seen anything since the wall blocks my view. I turned off the lights and went home."

"That must have been a shock to receive the call the next morning about what happened," I said.

"I was devastated."

"Was the maintenance man there when you two were bowling?" Jaxson asked.

"No. Gerald finished work at three. He needs to be here in the morning to make sure everything is in tip top condition for when we open."

I leaned forward. "If the front door was still unlocked, could someone have come in, killed Mr. Draper, and then left by the front entrance without your knowledge?" I asked.

"I'm assuming that is what happened."

That increased the suspect pool to anyone. So much for narrowing it down. I wish we knew if Dirk's diamonds were missing or not. Robbery could have been a motive.

I looked over at Carl. "If you can think of anyone who might want him dead, let us know." I started to stand.

"I can tell you who I think killed him."

My pulse soared, and I dropped down onto the seat. "Who?"

CHAPTER 8

If anyone knew who might have killed Diamond Dirk, it would have been the bowling alley manager. People in the service industry were often invisible to most people.

"Who do you suspect killed Diamond Dirk, Mr. Edwards?" I asked.

"Lanky Lou Owens."

I hadn't expected to hear that name, especially since he hadn't been at the bowling alley last night. On the other hand, Lucy's husband might have believed he was creating an alibi by saying he was sick. If he returned after the league night ended and killed Dirk, his wife, Lucy, would be crushed. My question was how could Lucy not have noticed that her sick husband wasn't home when she returned after the league? Or was she in on the murder too? So many options made my head spin.

"Why do you think that?" Jaxson asked the manager. I was glad he said something, since I was reeling from the news.

"Lou accused Dirk a few times of messing around with his wife."

Lanky Lou was no looker, but he was a sight better than

Diamond Dirk—even with the man's many jewels. "Do you think there is any truth to that?"

While I didn't spend a lot of time studying the interaction between Dirk and his teammates, I certainly didn't pick up on any budding romance between him and Lucy.

He shrugged. "I've heard rumors that Lucy wasn't completely happy in her marriage."

"Why is that, do you suppose?" Perhaps it would shed some light on what was going on.

"Lou had secrets."

Why did everything come down to that? When I was trying to find out who'd killed Morgan Oliver, his aunt said she'd left her husband because of all of his secrets.

"What kind of secrets?" Jaxson asked. My partner usually let me lead the investigation, but clearly, I wasn't on top of my game.

Carl chuckled. "Who knows? That's why they're called secrets. Besides, I try to keep out of everyone's affairs. That being said, since I occasionally bowl with Dirk, I hear things. That's all." He slapped his thighs. "Listen, I have a ton of stuff to do, what with the cops being here for much of the morning."

We had overstayed our visit. "Thanks for being so open with us."

"You bet."

Jaxson and I headed out. I was glad he didn't suggest we get in a game, because at the moment, my head wasn't in the right place.

As soon as I slipped into the car, I faced him. "Your thoughts?"

He started the engine. "Hard to say. His story seems consistent with the events."

"I thought that too. At first, I believed he would have heard a struggle, a grunt, or a yell, but with his door closed, it was surprisingly quiet." The falling of pins was a dull noise in the background.

"Which means we're back to square one," Jaxson said.

That was a bummer. "The next obvious person to speak with is Mrs. Draper."

Jaxson glanced over at me. "Why? She already confessed to your nail tech lady that she suspected her husband of cheating, which confirms what Carl Edwards said."

"True, though I would like to ask her if it was common for Dirk and Carl to bowl a game or two after league night ended."

He shot a glance at me. "You didn't believe him? He had enough plaques and trophies to prove he was good enough to go head-to-head with Dirk."

So many options were short-circuiting my logic. "I don't know what to think anymore—other than we need a white board for our office so I can jot down my thoughts—jumbled as they might be."

Jaxson laughed. "I hope you aren't planning on installing it on the wall across from the sofa where everyone can see it."

"Funny. No, I thought we could get a small table and place it across from the kitchen sink and then put a white board on it if you can't hang it." The wall was portable.

"I imagine I can figure something out. What would go on this board?"

"I'd list every person who was in the league, as well as people who came in contact with Dirk. Next to each name, I'd write my thoughts."

"Like a spreadsheet?"

"Yes, only you can add stuff too. As they say, two heads are better than one."

He flashed me a smile. "I like it. How about we go first thing tomorrow morning?"

"I told my aunt I'd work until noon. Corinne had a doctor's appointment."

"After that then. Stop on by and we'll go pick one up."

I appreciated that he liked to do things in a prompt fashion.

When I returned home, Iggy was pacing the floor. I couldn't tell if he was agitated or excited. "Hey, you. What's up?"

"You'll never guess who stopped over." From the excitement in his voice, it was someone good.

"Who?"

"Guess."

Only one thing would excite him this much. "Aimee."

"How did you know?"

I laughed. "Lucky guess. What did she want?"

"Just to talk. She even licked my nose."

Eww. "Is that a good thing?" Iguanas liked water, but cat saliva?

"Are you kidding? I took it to be like a kiss. You should try it sometime."

I laughed. "And which man should I be licking?"

"Humans don't lick. They kiss. Even I know that," Iggy said.

I'd go along with his little game as soon as I grabbed something to drink. Iggy followed me into the kitchen where I grabbed my pitcher of tea and poured a glass. "I'll ask again. Which man are you thinking I should be kissing?"

I held my breath, not certain what I wanted him to say.

"Unless you're holding out on me, there is one choice. Jaxson."

My pulse soared. "I'm not kissing my business partner." It didn't matter he was the subject of more than one of my dreams.

"Why not? He likes you."

"All the more reason I should keep my distance. We're business partners. What if Aimee said she wanted to move in here? Would you like that?" It was better to turn the tables on him.

"I'm not suggesting you and Jaxson get married tomorrow."

"I'm glad to hear it. While I appreciate the suggestion, I'm going to take things slow."

Iggy crawled up my leg and sat on my shoulder. "Trust me, Aimee is taking things slow, and it is driving me crazy."

"Welcome to the real world, Iggy."

He head butted my neck, and I laughed.

BECAUSE I HAD BEEN WORKING at the office for a few days in a row, my body decided it was normal to sleep in. When my alarm went off at five-forty-five, it came as a rude wake up call. I most definitely wasn't ready to rise and shine—but I did.

I muddled through the breakfast shift and was very happy when noon rolled around so I could leave. After I changed out of my costume, I headed over to the office. It was nice to find Jaxson at his desk, hard at work. "Hey," I said.

He looked up and smiled. "Ready to get that white board?"

"Absolutely. Maybe afterward, we can grab a bite to eat. I'm famished."

"Deal. Oh. Check this out." He lifted his pant leg.

"Pink socks. Are you kidding me? That's awesome."

Jaxson laughed. "Gotta go pink if I'm going to be a sleuth."

I grinned. "You got that right."

How cool was he? First the pink silicone bracelet and now pink socks. I wondered if he'd ever wear a pink shirt?

Naturally, Jax drove, but even a trip to the stationery store was not ordinary, because I was doing it with another person. I hadn't realized how much I'd miss the companionship.

We checked out a few sizes of boards and then both agreed on the six-foot by four-foot model.

Jaxson even found fasteners at the store with which to hang it. After I purchased some markers and an eraser, we headed back to the office, but not before we stopped at a fast food place for a quick bite.

"I need to check on Iggy first before I get to work," I said. I was curious if he was still floating on a cloud after their intimate touch yesterday.

"Go ahead. I'll hang this bad boy."

Bad boy? I laughed. "That would be great. Thank you."

"No problem."

I left by the inside stairwell. Drake was in the front conversing with a customer, so I slipped out the back and headed over to the Tiki Hut Grill. Just as I pulled open the door to the gift shop, who should be coming out but Penny. I hadn't realized it was time for her to get off work. Time really flew when I wasn't waitressing.

"Hey, fancy meeting you here," I said, happy to see her.

I expected a smile, but instead I received a sniffle. "I was just coming over to your office to find you."

"Oh, no. What's wrong?"

"Can we talk?"

"Absolutely. Let's go upstairs."

Together, we hiked up to my apartment. I said nothing, waiting for Penny to tell me what terrible tragedy had befallen her. Because she was kind of a drama queen, I had no idea what to expect.

When I entered, Iggy hopped down from his stool. "I'm bored and hungry."

I had to assume Aimee hadn't shown up today. That had to hurt. "I'm sorry. I'll get you something to eat, but even if you'd been with me at the office, you would have spent most of the day alone. Jax and I did a lot of running around."

"That's always your excuse." Iggy looked up at Penny. "You don't look so good."

"I feel even worse."

"Tell me about it," Iggy said. "My supposed girlfriend was really friendly yesterday and then didn't even had the decency to stop over today."

"Iggy," I said. "Life isn't always about you. Can't you see that Penny needs our attention?"

He looked between us and then lowered his head. "I guess."

"Why don't you go over to Aunt Fern's place? Maybe Aimee wants you to make the next move."

He perked up. "You think?"

"Go see." Sheesh. It was like raising a teenager. My only experience with that age group was when I taught middle school math for a year.

"Okay." Iggy rushed to the cat door, pushed it open, and jumped out.

It was a little after three, a bit too early to be enjoying a glass of wine. "Come into the kitchen while I grab us something to drink."

"It's Hunter."

If her ex-husband had messed up, I could handle it, but not Hunter. "What happened?"

"It's more like what didn't happen." She pulled out a kitchen chair and plopped down.

There were too many blanks to fill in. "I don't understand."

"I really, really like Hunter and want to get to know the man better, but every time I ask him where he came from, why he hunts at night, and stuff like that, he lies."

That was bad. "Does he know you can tell when someone isn't telling the truth?"

"No, and that's the problem. I don't want to accuse him of anything and chance losing him."

That was quite a dilemma. It never occurred to me not to tell Jaxson the truth. "What are you going to do?" I had no words of wisdom.

"Maybe you can do a truth spell on Hunter."

I laughed, only because that idea was so preposterous. "Me, put a spell on someone? Knowing my luck, Hunter would end up *only* being able to tell lies from here on out. Why don't you go to Hex and Bones and see what you'd have to do to put a spell on Hunter?"

"You know I don't do spells—at least I don't do them often. I'm more of a sense things kind of person."

Like an empath. "I get it."

I fixed us two glasses of iced tea and then motioned we return to the living room where it would be more comfortable than the hard, wooden kitchen chairs. We sat next to each other on the couch in our usual positions.

"Didn't you say Miriam told you that Gertrude gives lessons in spells?" she asked.

I blew out a breath. "I had totally forgotten about that, what with all the murders, but she apparently does."

"Why don't you see if you can improve your witch skills? You'd be a better sleuth if you could do a few more things."

I was convinced her suggestion was to get me to put an honesty spell on Hunter. As nice as that would be, the two of them needed to figure things out without witchcraft.

"I love that idea, but what if I mess things up even more? If I'm being paid by a client, I'm not about to put a spell on some unfaithful husband. It could prove disastrous."

Penny shook her head. "Haven't you heard the expression, 'Practice Makes Perfect'?"

"I think you mean, 'Perfect Practice Makes Perfect.' I'm not sure I'll ever get the hang of being a witch—at least as far as spells are concerned."

My friend grabbed my hand. "Since when do you give up?"

"You're right. Never."

"So there. Let's pretend Gertrude could guarantee success with your spells. What would you love to be able to do?"

I thought she'd come here to discuss her issues with Hunter. Maybe she was looking for a distraction. "I probably would try honing my telekinesis skills, but I would never use it to cheat." Under dire circumstances, Iggy could cloak himself, but his ability to hold the shield of invisibility was suspect. "I'd love to be able to become invisible so I could eavesdrop."

Penny waved a hand. "There you go. Ask Gertrude about putting up some kind of shield. All she can say is no."

My friend was right. I had to try. "I'll check it out. Now that you've solved my greatest desires, what can I do to help you—besides putting a spell on Hunter to reveal his deepest, darkest secrets to you?"

"You being here and listening to me is good enough. I'm hoping that with time, Hunter will come to realize that he can trust me."

Translated, she meant she didn't need any witchy help. "I think you might be right."

Once Penny left, I thought about checking up on Iggy, but I didn't want to embarrass him in case he and Aimee were having a good time. I returned to the office. The more I thought about taking those witch lessons, the more I liked the idea, but I wanted to pass it by Jaxson. He might have a moral issue with it.

When I entered the office, he was sitting at his desk, typing something on his computer. He looked up and nodded toward the kitchen that was situated behind the portable wall. "Check it out."

"You installed the white board already?" I was so excited.

"Yup."

I raced around the wall, checked out the board, and grinned. "This is great!" I called.

As much as I wanted to start writing on it, I needed to discuss the idea of me taking witch lessons. I walked back into the main office. "Thank you."

"No problem. How was Iggy?"

"Hungry and bored, until I suggested he go visit Aimee." I explained about the possible shared kiss yesterday.

"A kiss? Sweet. Go Iggy."

I laughed. "Oh, and I ran into Penny. For reasons I'll skip for the moment, she came up with a suggestion." I explained about the classes on doing spells. "What do you think?"

"If you can become invisible, people will travel across the state to hire us."

Unexpected relief poured through me. Jaxson was the best. "No guarantee I'll get this right, but I want to try. I owe it to our company."

"You only owe it to yourself."

When did he get so philosophical? "How about I speak with Gertrude and then maybe we can grab an early dinner?"

I hoped I wasn't being too presumptuous to think he wanted to spend every minute with me, but we had things to discuss.

"Sounds good. See if Gertrude is free. I'm in the middle of doing a little research, and I want to finish."

Because I was so happy, I almost leaned over and kissed

him, but of course, I didn't. "On what? Or should I say on whom?"

"I'm not finished researching everything yet. I'll tell you when you get back."

Everyone had his secrets. Sheesh. "Later."

It was a lovely afternoon, and I enjoyed the walk over to the Psychics Corner. I should have called to make an appointment with Gertrude, but I didn't mind waiting if she was busy. It wasn't as if I didn't have a lot to think about. If she had gone home for the day, I'd make an appointment for tomorrow.

It turned out that I only had to wait about twenty minutes before Sarah ushered me into the psychic's office. Gertrude looked up from her desk. "Glinda, nice to see you again."

I was always in awe when I was around her. Growing up, I'd heard many wonderful stories about her abilities. "Nice to see you too."

"Have a seat and tell me how I can help you." She rose from behind her desk and eased her way over to the chair next to the sofa.

"Miriam said you hold classes for witches. I'd love to sign up for one as I need to hone my spell abilities."

Her eyes widened. "I used to give classes, but I don't anymore."

My spine crumbled. I didn't realize how much I had wanted to be a good witch. Perhaps if the spell I tried to do on Iggy hadn't failed, I wouldn't be so disappointed. "Oh."

"Is there a particular spell you want to be able to perform? A love spell per chance?" Her eyes twinkled.

I barked out a laugh. Love spell indeed. "No. Since Iggy can cloak himself, at least for a small period of time, I would love to be able to do that too. To be a fly on a wall could help my chances at succeeding as a sleuth."

Gertrude shook her head. "That is very difficult to do."

I bet she meant to say that for a witch of my caliber it would be almost impossible. "Can you cloak yourself?"

I swear her cheeks turned pink. "I can, but I've had years of practice."

Yes! That meant it was possible. "Can you show me? Even if I could stay invisible for a few seconds, that would be great."

She inhaled, her gaze boring into mine.

CHAPTER 9

"Here's the thing, Glinda," Gertrude said. "Not all spells are created equally. I don't cloak myself anymore, because it takes a tremendous amount of energy to do so. Perform it too often, and it might damage your body."

That sounded terrible, but I was only twenty-six, not almost ninety like Gertrude. Surely, I could handle it. I didn't want to consider going to a gym and building my strength just to be a better sleuth, but if it meant I'd be a success, I would consider it.

"I'd still like you to teach me to do it. I mean, if some unscrupulous person became upset because I was asking too many questions, and he pulled a gun on me, it would be in my best interest if I could disappear. Right?"

Her lips lifted. "Yes, dear. It would definitely be worth it in that case." Gertrude stood and walked over to her bookcase. After a minute of searching, she pulled out a book. Once seated, she flipped through it. "Here it is."

She handed it to me. Sure enough, it was a spell to block light from bouncing off a person's image while reflecting the images behind the person to the front. "This would make me invisible?"

"Completely."

The spell was ten lines long, most of which made little sense. It would take a while to memorize the words. I turned to the next page. "What is the spell to stop being invisible?"

"There isn't one. It will slowly wear off."

That was kind of creepy. "Can a person hear me if I speak?"

"Yes, dear. You are really there. It only seems as if you are not. That means if someone took a swing at you, trust me, you'd feel it, and so would their fist."

It was better than nothing. "Will I need candles, herbs, or eye of newt?"

"Nothing like that. You'll just need to copy the spell."

This was too good to be true. "Can I ask you for one or two more spells?"

"Of course."

Jaxson wanted to be able to understand Iggy. I thought that was really cool, but I wanted us to be more on an equal footing than we already were—which is where the second spell came in. "Is there a spell that can help a human hear a witch's familiar?"

"There is."

My pulse soared. "And secondly, is there something I can do to give a man excellent hearing and/or super sharp eyesight, like an animal would possess?"

"Why, yes there is!"

"How did it go?" Jaxson asked when I returned to the office.

I smiled. "I flickered."

He closed his laptop and studied me. "You flickered? What on Earth does that mean?"

I pulled my chair from behind my desk and placed it in front of his. I then pulled out a piece of paper that I'd copied the spell on. "She gave me a spell to recite when I want to become invisible."

"Invisible?"

Why did people insist on repeating what I said? "In truth, all it does is allow me to absorb the light around me so I can't be seen while projecting all images behind me to the front. Mind you, there are problems associated with this—mainly it takes a lot of energy."

"Interesting. How long could you hold the spell?"

"Since I've not really done it but one time—albeit briefly —I can't say. I'm thinking not long, which is why I have to practice it. Before I do though, I want to do something for you."

He leaned back. "For me? What is it?"

"How would you like to have super hearing and super eyesight?" I would incorporate the spell for him to hear Iggy at the same time since the two spells were related.

His mouth opened and then shut. "Like an animal's?"

"Yes."

Jackson blew out a breath. "I'd be willing to wear a lot of pink for that."

I laughed. "Do you want to try it? According to Gertrude, there aren't any side effects, other than enhanced senses." And being subjected to Iggy's sass for the rest of his life.

Jaxson grinned. "Let's do it."

"I need you to sit across from me."

We could have sat on the sofa, but it would be easier if his chair faced mine. I placed the paper on my lap as he moved into position.

"Now what?"

"This might sound a bit strange, but you need to hold my pink diamond pendant in your hand while I'm wearing it. Gertrude said it will connect us since I draw power from it."

I lifted my necklace out from under my shirt. When he grabbed hold, his knuckles brushed my skin, and my heart fluttered at the intimate touch. It was a stupid reaction since he was just following my instructions. It meant nothing.

Jaxson nodded at the paper on my lap. "Do I need to recite anything?"

"No. I have to say it, but first I'll place my hands over your closed eyes, say the first three lines of the spell, and then I'll gently cup your ears and finish the spell."

"That's it?"

"Yes."

"How long will it last?" he asked.

"Gertrude said it depends on the recipient. The stronger the person's energy, the longer it will last."

Jaxson nodded. "I have no idea what that means, but I'm game."

He might be, but I wasn't sure if I was. I prayed it didn't blind him or make him deaf instead. Witchcraft could be tricky, but I trusted Gertrude. She would have warned me about this spell if it was dangerous.

I placed my palms over his eyes and tried to forget that we were this close to each other. Hopefully, he couldn't hear my heart beating fast—yet. I glanced down at the paper and read the words silently to make sure I could do this. Gertrude said there was no need for candles or herbs, which I found strange, but who was I to question the master?

I inhaled and began the spell. The foreign words made no sense to me. They appeared to be in some kind of Old English. Why couldn't today's great witches write new spells for us newbies in an easy to understand language?

Once I finished with the phrases, I moved my hands to

his ears. "Keep your eyes closed," I told him. That wasn't part of the spell, but I didn't need him watching me.

I could do this. Only a few more sentences to plow through. Not wanting to disturb the all-powerful spell witches in the sky—assuming they even existed—I spoke slowly and softly. Once I finished, I lowered my hands, and exhaled.

"You can let go of my necklace and open your eyes."

When he did, Jaxson said nothing, his brown eyes focused solely on me. "Say something," he said.

"Hello?"

"I'm too close. " Jaxson shoved back his chair. "We need to do a different test. I'm going into the bathroom and closing the door. When you hear the latch click, speak in a normal conversational tone."

"I can do that."

Once Jaxson reached his destination, I asked if he could hear me. A second later, he burst out of the room with a grin so wide, I thought it would split his face in two. "That was incredible."

He rushed to the window that overlooked the ocean, most likely to check out his vision.

"Can you see better?" I asked.

"I can't tell. Come here." I stepped next to him. "See that woman in the red bathing suit holding a book?" he asked.

The book was tiny. "Yes."

"What's the title?"

I laughed. "I couldn't see that even with binoculars." Or probably a telescope.

"I can. It's called Murder with a Muffin."

"Seriously. That's the real title?"

He spun to face me. "No, but I could see the word *murder*. This is beyond wonderful."

He drew me into a hug, lifted me up, and spun me

around. I was almost too stunned to enjoy the intimate contact. For sure, the man had pecs of steel. He set me down.

I'd never seen him this excited before. For his sake, I hoped his enhanced senses lasted for days or even weeks. I wasn't all that confident, because if any witch could do that spell, they would be in high demand for the service. I didn't want to dampen his enthusiasm and tell him about his possible ability to hear Iggy. One step at a time.

"Let's work on you being invisible. I am stoked about your new witch abilities."

I grabbed a hold of his shoulders. "It really uses a lot of energy. Nothing in the witch world is without consequences."

"Okay, but you might need to disappear someday. Don't you want to know if you can do it?"

For our company to succeed, I had to have talents that the sheriff's department didn't. "Okay, I'm game."

"Can I say the spell?" Jaxson asked.

"You can recite it, but since you aren't a witch, it won't do any good."

"That's no fun."

I walked over to the sofa and sat down. I flipped over the paper to read the other spell. Having minored in physics, I had my doubts this could work, but if Iggy and Gertrude could do it, why couldn't I?

When I tried it before, Gertrude said I was invisible for only a second, but that was because I wasn't concentrating hard enough. Practice did seem to play a role. Determined to succeed for a few seconds at least, I inhaled and focused.

At some point I would memorize the words, but until then, I'd have to read them. If this worked, I'd type them into my phone in case I needed the spell when I was out and about.

I grabbed hold of my magical stone just as Gertrude had

instructed and whispered the spell. For it to be effective in an emergency, I needed it to work by mentally reciting it or mouthing the words.

I read them out loud this time. The second I finished, what felt like a sharp, hot wave passed through me.

"Glinda?" Jaxson asked.

I glanced down at my body—or rather where my body used to be. Oh. My. Goodness. I did it! "I'm here," I said in as normal a voice as I could.

"I hear you." He slowly moved toward me on the sofa, probably afraid he might sit on me. He reached out. "I'm trying to touch you."

I grabbed his hand, and he jerked it back. "Sorry. That must have felt creepy."

"It did, kind of."

Since I couldn't reverse the spell, I had to wait it out. A horrific idea shot to mind. I was Glinda Goodall, the witch who messed up everything. What if I never reappeared?

As if that thought broke the spell, I became visible again. I looked up at Jaxson. He touched my leg. "You're back," he announced.

I thought it obvious, but I imagine all of this witch stuff could be rather disconcerting to the uninitiated. "I am."

"How do you feel?"

"I was only invisible for a short period of time, so I doubt there will be any lasting effects." I stood and instantly dropped back onto the sofa, my legs too weak to hold me. I hadn't expected that reaction. No wonder Gertrude didn't want to be invisible for more than a few seconds. Apparently, she'd mastered the ability to reappear at will.

"How about getting me some water?" I asked, needing a moment to myself.

"Sure."

Jax rushed to do my bidding. He returned with a glass and

held it out to me. "Drink this. Then we're going to eat. You need the energy."

This time I didn't disagree. The water helped. Jaxson insisted he help me up. In truth, his aid was welcome.

"Go slow," he said, acting like I was an invalid. Okay, I was weak. As soon as I ate, I was sure I'd be back to normal. The ability to disappear was so revolutionary that it could make our sleuthing firm the best in the state.

"Where do you want to eat?" he asked.

"How about someplace on the edge of town? For once, I'd rather not run into a gossip queen."

"I agree."

CHAPTER 10

We were seated at a small cafe about three miles outside of the town's limit. I'd never been to the Sunshine Café before, but it was really cute and would afford us some privacy. It seemed as if all of the eating establishments on the main drag of Witch's Cove were owned by the gossip queens—all except the small restaurant at the Magic Wand Hotel. I'd spoken to the owners, Ted and Nate Bellows, a few times in the past, but it seemed as if they were always busy, running around attending to guests, preventing any time for gossiping.

"Tell me what had Penny so upset," Jaxson said. We'd already ordered and were waiting for our meals to arrive.

"She thinks Hunter is lying to her."

"Oh, yeah? About what?"

"She wasn't specific. I think it's about why he isn't always available to be with her," I said. "He uses the excuse of needing to be in the woods quite often."

"Isn't he the forest ranger? Maybe he needs to be there."

"Yes, but I doubt his office hours extend past sunset."

But what did I know? I still was unsure why anyone would give crossbow lessons at night either.

"That does seem odd, but to be honest, they barely know each other. I wouldn't worry about it just yet. If a man's been burned by a woman, he might want to be cautious the next go around."

That was intriguing. "Are you speaking from experience?"

"Sweetheart, you know all my dirty laundry. If I haven't told you something, it's because I figured Drake had already filled you in."

"Probably true." I inhaled, happy to know that. "Most likely Hunter just needs some breathing room from being with Penny all the time."

"I agree. I've learned that if one member of the dating team is interested in moving faster than the other person, it can be a bit daunting."

"I can see that." I hoped he wasn't talking about us. I like things the way they were.

"If they are meant to be together, things will work out." Jaxson looked straight at me, but I immediately glanced around. I wasn't good with expressing my emotions.

"True."

Our food arrived, and it couldn't have come soon enough. I was starving. We both dug in.

"Good call," Jaxson said after he finished swallowing. "While you were with Gertrude, I found out something about Tinfoil Tim and his possible motive for murder."

I nearly choked on my food. "And you're telling me this now, why?"

His eyes widened. "You doing your spell was far more important than what I found out."

I had to admit, I was pretty stunned myself that I had been able to pull off not one, but two, spells successfully—or would it be three? "Tell me."

"Tinfoil Tim and Diamond Dirk had a history together."

"History?" I said. "Dirk just moved to town."

"I'm guessing here, but they probably met at the bowling alley. Tim was interested in starting a business of manufacturing satellite dishes. For that, he needed a warehouse. He found one for sale, and then went to Diamond Dirk—his good bowling buddy slash realtor."

I could fill in the rest. "Don't tell me Dirk botched the deal?"

"I'm afraid so. The details online were sketchy, but Dirk forgot to file some papers and the owner sold it to someone else. Tim sued Dirk."

I whistled. "I wonder how that lawsuit is going?"

Jaxson smiled. "I was wondering the same thing, so I called the courthouse. Apparently, last week the courts decided in favor of Dirk."

I whistled. "I bet Tim was a tad upset, but was it enough to murder the guy? I mean, why not buy another warehouse?"

Jaxson shrugged. "I couldn't say."

I mentally ran through the suspects again. "If we think the killer is a man, that leaves us with Tim, because he thinks Dirk swindled him somehow, and Lanky Lou, because he thinks Dirk and his wife were having an affair. I probably would have dismissed it if Dirk's wife didn't think it might be true."

"Don't forget that Dirk is on the winning team," Jaxson said. "Tim might have needed to be the top dog."

"True. Tim seems to be a bowling fanatic, as well as something of a conspiracy theorist when it comes to aliens."

"I agree. If we are going with the idea it needs to be someone strong enough to wield a bowling ball, what about Hemsworth, the body builder?" Jaxson threw out.

"What is his motive?"

"That is something we'd have to figure out," Jaxson said.

For the next few minutes, we ate in silence. Something about Carl Edwards, the manager, seemed off, but killing Dirk would be bad press for his bowling alley. It didn't matter if he was just the manager and not the owner. Bowling was his livelihood. "The only bowling person we haven't mentioned is Touring Tom." I couldn't remember his real name.

"I have no idea who he is, but I'll check into him. What about other real estate people? Dirk might have stolen a client or two out from under someone."

"If we want to know that, we'd have to ask Lucy Owens. Since she thinks we are looking to buy a home, I doubt she'd talk to us if we tell her the truth."

"Good point. We'll have to figure out something else."

Even though I appreciated that Jaxson was willing to put in long hours, he shouldn't have to. Once we finished, I pulled out my credit card to pay. "I need some down time to figure this out. I feel as if the killer is staring us in the face, but I can't see him."

"It's possible we've spoken to him already."

I snapped my fingers. "Possibly, but we've not met Lucy's husband, Lou. I'll see if I can find out where he works and figure out if I can talk to him tomorrow."

"Nuh-uh. We agreed that talking to potential killers is dangerous," Jaxson said. "I'll come with you."

"You are sweet. Tomorrow is Sunday, so maybe I'll do a little research and start again on Monday."

"Make sure you don't go without me."

"I won't." I wasn't stupid. Even with the ability to cloak myself, I wasn't sure I would chance it.

"The wine shop also is closed then so I have time to do a bit of research."

That would work out well since I wanted to spend some

time with Aunt Fern to find out how her romance with Bob Hatfield was going. Entering the dating scene for her after so many years had to be strange. She and Bob had only been on a couple of dates, but I was curious what her opinion of him was. Last time I asked, she said she hadn't made up her mind.

PARTLY BECAUSE I needed the money and partly because waitressing might stimulate the creative side of my brain, I took an early morning shift. I used to have Sundays off, but since I was no longer a regular, I didn't care when I worked.

Penny was there, and she seemed to be her usual chipper self. I guess she had come to grips with her relationship with Hunter. Needing to chat, I intercepted her coming out from the kitchen area.

"How's it going with the new girl?" I asked.

"Donna will never be you."

"I hope not. And Hunter? Did you talk to him last night?"

She grinned. "I did. In fact, he came over and brought me dinner. We had a great time!" She glanced at the ceiling and sighed.

I liked the sound of that, but this wasn't the time or place to ask for details. "I'm glad. I'm sure if the man has any secrets, he'll eventually tell you."

"You know, I've been thinking," Penny said in that tone I recognized as one that would get us in trouble.

"About?"

"Hunter is giving lessons tomorrow night in the forest. I thought maybe we could..."

"We could what?" This sounded bad.

"Watch?"

I chuckled. "You mean spy?"

"You know you want to do it. Your dad will be with him. This will be your chance to see him in action."

Darn her. Penny understood my curiosity about some things was a thirst that could never be quenched. "Let me think about it. I'd want Jaxson to come just in case we twist an ankle, or something bad is going on there."

She laughed. "You want him there because you like him."

There was no use arguing. "I do like Jax. A lot. But he and I are work partners. Nothing more." Sheesh. She sounded like Iggy, always pushing us together.

"It could be more, right?"

The chef shouted my order was ready. Good timing. "Duty calls."

"Think about it," Penny said.

"I will."

For the rest of my shift, I pictured myself finally learning what my dad was up to. If he caught us, though, he'd be either embarrassed or mad. I bet Iggy would be up for a little reconnaissance though. Aunt Fern had made him a camouflaged outfit for Halloween last year. The hoodie covered half of his body and head. His pink face, legs, and tail were totally exposed, however. Because I had gone as my nemesis, the Wicked Witch of the West, last October, I'd purchased green face paint. An idea formed—one that just might work.

After I made sure all of my tables were taken care of, I caught Aunt Fern alone.

"How did it go with your date last night?" I asked.

She lifted a shoulder "Bob is a nice man. We went to one of his hospital parties that was very fancy. It was a cancer fundraiser."

"That sounds like fun, but you don't seem exactly over the moon about him."

She blew out a breath. "Oh, Glinda. I do like him, but he's

made some comments about my hair being a bit, what did he say, too stodgy for him."

"Stodgy? Ouch." Her curly hair was hard to style, which might be why she usually wore her fairy godmother crown to keep it tamed.

Mind you, when my aunt dressed up, she wasn't authentic to any one style. She had a tendency to mix and match movie heroines, which might be a bit off-putting to a hospital administrator.

"Bob often mentions Ann, his wife, and how she used to wear her hair and how fashionable she was."

Warning bells sounded in my brain. "Doesn't that bother you?"

"Of course, it does," Aunt Fern shot back.

"Have you spoken to him about it?"

She glanced to the side. "Not yet."

"Why? Because you're afraid he'll not want to go out with you again?"

"Maybe," she mumbled. "I'm not sure I'm ready to be a wife replacement."

"Nor should you want to be. Changing anything about yourself to please another is wrong on so many levels."

I had to say that Jaxson never once asked that I not wear pink. For that, he would have a good place in my heart.

"You are so right."

"What are you going to do?" I didn't want her to dump Bob because of anything I said though.

"Sleep on it."

"Sounds good. By the way, do you think you could whip up some pink curtains for my office some time? No rush."

She smiled. "It would be my pleasure. Just give me the measurements and I'll get right on it."

"You are the best."

"Just promise that when the office is finished, you'll invite me over."

"Absolutely." I think a party would definitely be in order.

EVEN THOUGH I was up and about the next morning by eight, when I arrived at the office, Jaxson was there—wearing a pink shirt.

"This is becoming a pink trend," I announced with probably too much cheer in my voice.

He grinned. "It doesn't make me look fat does it?"

He was mocking me since I was always asking him that question. "You look very masculine and hot."

Heat raced up my face at that comment—a comment that had just slipped out.

His eyes widened. "Thank you. I might have to start wearing pink every day."

I laughed. "I fear our future clients might think it a bit weird if we matched."

"Got it. I'll be more subtle with my pink choices next time."

He was the best. "Did you find out anything last night?" I asked.

"I did. I went on a social media hunt and learned that Tim Bowers works from home doing design work for an electronics firm. And yes, I have his address. As for Lou Owens, or Lanky Lou as we know him, he works on a road crew. I imagine he'll be home around three-ish, since crews often start their day very early to avoid the heat."

"You have been productive."

He nodded. "Have you come up with any more suspects?"

"No. I checked the website where both Dirk and Lucy

worked, and their employees are either female or one rather old man. Unless the coroner can provide us with more information, it looks like we've narrowed it down to a few."

"Just to be thorough, I checked into Carl Edwards, the manager. The guy has quite a number of impressive tournament wins."

"Good to know he was telling the truth. It's a shame he has arthritis. That has to be tough working in a bowling alley when you'd rather be competing. I have to say that he doesn't look old enough to have that disease."

"I've heard it can strike at any age," Jaxson said.

"Sad. Since I'd like to learn a bit more about Lanky Lou before we speak to him—or Tinfoil Tim for that matter—I think I'll have a chat with our bookstore owners. I've purchased so many books from them, I'm sure Betty would be willing to give me her opinion on who might have wanted Dirk dead."

"Great. I think you can handle them yourself, right?"

I laughed. "Totally."

Both Betty and Frank were older than my parents. They'd have no reason to kill anyone.

CHAPTER 11

Before I got into the sleuthing business, when I wanted to learn something, I would pretend to browse in a store or order something simple at a restaurant. If Jaxson and I were to succeed, however, people needed to know that we were there for information—information that we wouldn't share with anyone. The sheriff didn't believe in second-hand gossip, so there would be no need to tell him.

The moment I walked into the bookstore my blood pressure immediately dropped. I loved the smell of paper and old leather, and this ancient store did not disappoint. The Candles Bookstore had a used section that housed books dating back to the late eighteen-hundreds. In the front of the store sat the new releases. Off to the side was an assortment of handmade candles, greeting cards, and calendars. I wasn't sure who bought a calendar this late in the year, but maybe there was a market for it.

Betty Sanchez strolled over to me. "Glinda. This is a nice surprise. Can I help you find something?"

"Not exactly. You know me, I can't let something go when I start thinking about it."

She smiled. "You are tenacious. Don't tell me you're here about Dirk's murder? I heard you and Jaxson Harrison opened up your own investigation firm."

She was observant—and a gossip. Good. "Yes, we did." Since I feared she'd want to know why I decided to open the firm and why I chose Jaxson as my partner, I wanted to ask my questions as quickly as I could. "I didn't even know Dirk Draper, but considering someone stuffed a pink bowling pin in his mouth, I have a sense that someone is trying to frame *me* for his murder." Surely, that detail had made the rounds already. I didn't believe someone was trying to frame me, but it might open her up.

"I am so sorry this is happening to you. I guess the fact the bowling pin was pink would be something you'd use—assuming you were a killer." She tittered.

"Maybe, but I wouldn't be stupid enough to leave a calling card like that. Do you have any ideas who might have done this?" My pulse sped up.

"Why no. Do you?"

Drat. I didn't want to give her my rundown of suspects in case she decided to blab. One of the reasons I came in here today was because I was looking for someone to give me some gossip—not the other way around.

"Not really. I don't know enough about anyone." I inhaled. "Rumor has it, though, that Lanky Lou was upset with Dirk because Lucy and Dirk were...you know."

She waved a hand. "No way. Lucy has better taste than that."

If she said so. "Why would Lou think that then?"

"I couldn't say, but if you ask him, be careful. He has a temper."

"I'll keep that in mind. If Lou believes his wife is cheating, maybe she was with someone else," I offered.

"Like with who?"

"What about Carl, the manager?"

She laughed. "Why would you think that? He's married for one thing."

So was Lucy—and Dirk for that matter—but I hadn't heard that about the manager. I needed to find some dirt on one of the players. "How about Tinfoil Tim? Did he have a beef with Dirk?"

She pointed a finger at me. "He's my bet."

"Why is that?"

Betty looked around the empty store. Maybe she thought she'd heard someone had come in. "Tim prides himself on being the best player. When Diamond Dirk came to town, he was not happy."

"There's always someone better waiting in the wings. I don't see that as motive for murder."

"Maybe not, but Dirk told Tim that he wanted to sponsor him for some tournament." Betty lifted her chin.

That was news. I waited for her to fill me in, but she didn't. "And?"

"Dirk bailed. Said some real estate venture he thought would come through didn't happen, and he didn't have the cash readily available."

I'd be bummed too, if that ever happened. If he was hard up for cash, maybe he had failed to pay alimony or child support. If one of Dirk's ex-wives had remarried, perhaps one of their husbands had gone after Dirk. Oh, boy. The suspects were mounting.

"Was Tim ever violent?" I asked. "Like if he didn't get that strike, did he smash his ball on anything?"

"Heavens no. That ball was like his child. That doesn't mean he couldn't have killed Dirk. Tim is cuckoo."

"Because he believed in aliens?" I asked.

"Yes. He claims to have been abducted too. The aliens did

experiments on him. He said it was terrible. It's why he wears his tinfoil hat."

"If that happened to me, I might wear protective gear too. But just because a person has notions different from others, doesn't mean he's a killer."

Clearly, Betty was a bit prejudiced in this department.

"Talk to Produce Polly. She knows him better than anyone." That was code for *we're done here*.

"I just might. And thanks for the chat. If I hadn't promised Jaxson we'd look into a few things, I'd spend an hour browsing." That was bogus, but I needed to say something, or I'd end up spending what money I had on books. I have an addiction to them.

"Come again when you have a chance to see our new selections," Betty said.

"I will."

When I left, I was more torn than ever. Since tonight was a full moon, I decided it was time to find out where my father was going some nights—even if that meant I had to stop snooping for one day. As far as I knew, no one was trying to frame me for the murder, so I was free to take some time off. If Steve or Nash thought I was a viable suspect, they would be camped on my doorstep, ready to drag me to jail.

Since I needed to tell Jaxson my plan to help Penny tonight, I stopped back at our office. Knowing him, he'd want to join us. In truth, I needed him. If he had super eyesight and super hearing—assuming he still possessed it—I wanted him to come. My goal for this mission was to see whether my dad was taking crossbow lessons at night with Hunter, or if he was involved in something else. My intuitive side was telling me I wouldn't find my father with any kind of weapon in his hand, but the only way to know for sure was to spy.

To my surprise, Jaxson was not in the office when I

arrived. I checked downstairs and found him in the storage room loading wine onto the shelves. I smiled. It was like old times. "Hey."

He set down the case. "How did it go at the bookstore?"

I told him everything Betty said, including my thoughts that if Dirk's assets weren't liquid that maybe he failed to pay alimony or child support.

"Good thought. I'll see if I can find anything, but I won't hack into bank accounts. That's Steve's job."

"I agree. We already have three motives for Tim wanting Dirk dead."

"What's wrong," Jaxson asked. "I know that look."

"I'm not sure that's enough. It's all based on rumor."

He chuckled. "You're sounding like our sheriff in search of absolute proof. What if Tim thought Dirk was an alien come to harm him? Huh?"

My pulse soared. "That never occurred to me. Do you think he might have?"

Jaxson laughed. "I'm kidding you."

"Maybe not. Who knows what Tim is really thinking. I—I mean we—could visit him and ask."

Jaxson shook his head. "Even if we did, I don't think he'd admit something like that, assuming he's the killer."

"True, but other than Lanky Lou, who's left?" I asked.

"That's the problem. We are running out of options."

I blew out a breath. "I think we need to wait and see what the autopsy reveals."

He nodded. "The autopsy might narrow the field, but I'm skeptical. The doctor said he was hit in the back of the head with a bowling ball. What more can she tell us?"

"The angle? It might make a difference if the strike was to the top of the head or lower on the back of the head. That would tell us if Dirk was bending over, sitting, or maybe even lying on the floor. For all we know, he could have been killed with a knife. To frame someone, or to mess up the crime scene, the killer could have smashed his head in."

"Wow. How do you sleep at night?" he asked with a cute smirk.

"What do you mean?"

"Your mind never stops working, does it?"

"Sadly, no." Now to bring up the real reason I was there. "By the way, there is a full moon tonight."

Jaxson froze. "Don't tell me you plan to spy on your dad?"

He knew me too well. Okay, I might have mentioned that was my plan for about a week now. "I'm worried about him."

Jaxson chuckled. "Keep telling yourself that, sweetheart. It's killing you to not know what he's been up to." Jaxson led me out to the back room. "Tell me this. If you find out that he is merely taking hunting lessons, how will you react?"

"I'll be happy."

"Really?"

Okay, I hadn't thought this through. "I'll be happy he's doing what he wants to do, even if it's against what he's always believed in. I'll also be happy he wasn't lying. Not only that, Hunter will have been telling the truth to Penny—at least for much of it."

"Fine. And if you find out he isn't in the woods learning to use his crossbow, but Hunter and several others are?"

A knot formed in the pit of my stomach. "I will not assume he is cheating. I might have to confront him about it though. If I do, I hope my dad will come clean."

"What if he is doing something illegal? You said the funeral home isn't raking in the dough."

My stomach flipped again. "He wouldn't do that. He'd ask Aunt Fern for a loan first or grovel in front of his brothers for help." My mind tried to come up with other options. "I wouldn't be surprised if he is taking dancing lessons so he could surprise my mom for her birthday. She loves to dance."

Jaxson's eyebrows rose in disbelief as he held up a hand. "Fair enough. Last case scenario. Suppose he is in the woods with Hunter, but he isn't there to hunt. You've been hinting at the rather outlandish scenario that your father is some kind of werewolf. I personally am not a believer, but then again, I didn't believe in witches until I met you."

Light-headedness attacked me, and I grabbed onto the counter to keep from fainting. "I don't want to find out that full moon creatures of the night exist, or that my father is one of them, but if he is, I'll try to help him."

Jaxson crossed his arms. "If you do go to the Hendrian Forest, you'll need to be prepared for all three options."

"I know. I wish I could say I'll forget about the nonsense, but I know myself. I am eternally curious."

"You think?" Jaxson winked.

That action did more to lift my spirits than anything he could have said. "Funny. Just so you know, I plan to take Iggy with me and have him look around, so I won't get caught."

"He's pink. Won't he be seen from a mile around?"

"That's why I'm going to dress him up in camouflage and paint his face and extremities green."

Jaxson laughed. "He'll look like a Navy Seal—only a lot smaller."

"That's the point. I figure with your excellent hearing and sharp eyesight, I can keep out of the way—assuming you'll come with me."

"You know I will. And Penny? Do you think she'll want to find out the truth about Hunter?"

"She claims she does."

It was still early, but it would take me a while to get Iggy's outfit ready—as well as my own. Aunt Fern had already done the hard part of making the body of the outfit. I just needed to make a few adjustments. I even knew where some extra camouflage material was located.

"Good luck. What time do you want to head out?" Jaxson asked.

I had expected some backlash from him, telling me I was being ridiculous, but Jaxson didn't do any of that. Once more, I was eternally grateful to have him as my partner.

"Normally, I would ask my mom what time dad takes his lessons, but I don't want her to ask too many questions. How about nine o'clock? It will be dark by then."

"Sounds good. I'll drive."

I expected nothing less. "We'll be ready."

CHAPTER 12

Once back at the Tiki Hut, I went into the storage room and found the camouflage material I'd purchased for the Memorial Day festivities. I didn't need more than half a yard to do what I needed to. I debated asking Aunt Fern to help, but I kind of wanted to keep my spying venture quiet. She might have felt obligated to tell her brother-in-law what was going on. If Dad learned of my plan, he'd for sure stay away from the forest—unless he really was learning how to shoot a crossbow.

I located a pair of scissors in the bin, along with the material and some thread. I cut off a chunk and then went upstairs to create my masterpiece. Convincing Iggy to do this would be a no-brainer. It would be the highlight of his year.

After I made the additions to his costume, I planned to snag Penny when she got off work to make sure she still could join us.

As soon as I entered the apartment, Iggy jumped down from his stool. "What is that for?"

"Give me a sec, and I'll tell you." I went into my room,

located his Halloween outfit and carried it out. It was a bit smaller than I remembered.

"Aren't we a little early for Halloween?" he asked.

"It's for a mission that I'm going on tonight—an undercover mission where you will be the star."

Iggy bounced up and down and then did two circles before stopping. "Tell me everything."

I outlined my plan of driving to the park and then walking in on foot. "I don't imagine Hunter and his class will venture too far into the woods. With your excellent hearing, you can guide us."

"I'm in, but what is with the extra material?"

"This outfit needs to cover your tail and legs. I have green face paint to complete the disguise."

"Yippee. I'm going to tell Aimee."

"No!"

He stopped in his tracks. "Why not?"

"I'm not sure what we will find, and I'd rather not have Aunt Fern know just yet. Tomorrow will be soon enough. Besides, you'll be able to tell Aimee how you saved the day."

I was telling him what he wanted to hear, because I needed Iggy to go along with everything.

"That's dope."

"What?"

"I heard someone say it. It means it's really cool."

Now I felt old. "How did it go with Aimee today?"

"We're cool. For now. I don't really trust her."

I chuckled. "Relationships are hard. Be honest with her, and she'll come around."

"At the moment, she's good."

I smiled. "I'm happy to hear it."

It took about an hour to measure, cut, and hand sew his outfit. Once I finished, I had to say, it was *dope*. The edges weren't finished off, but Iggy wasn't on this mission to look good. My goal was to make sure the material covered all of him—including his tail. I doubt the bow at the top to keep the material in place was comfortable, but he might be too excited to notice. With the addition of some makeup, no one would see him in the forest. Worst case, he could climb a tree, assuming the material didn't affect his balance.

It was almost three, which meant it was time to talk to Penny. "I'll be right back."

Iggy was wearing his costume, prancing around, getting used to the feel. "I'm glad I don't have to wear my pink bowtie."

"There is that!"

"Are you sure I can't show Aimee?" he asked.

"Not yet."

"Spoilsport."

I laughed, glad to see my familiar in good spirits. I went downstairs and waited for Penny to finish her shift. When she was done, she rushed up to me. "What's up?"

"Can we talk?" I didn't want to be anywhere near Aunt Fern when I mentioned my desire to spy on my dad.

"Sure. I just need to clock out."

Once she finished, Penny followed me upstairs. "I've decided to go to the forest with you to spy on Hunter and my dad, assuming you're still game."

"Are you kidding? Of course, I am."

"Good. Jaxson and I will be leaving at nine."

"Jaxson and you, huh? We're getting pretty cozy, aren't we?" she asked with too much joy in her voice.

"Now isn't the time for that discussion. I need him there." I reminded her of the spell I put on him. "His hearing is still super sharp. Since I would appreciate no one knowing that I was there, I'm hoping we won't have to get too close to see what's going on. Besides, I have Iggy, the super sleuth." I told her about the spell that would enable Jaxson to communicate with Iggy. "I haven't told him since it probably didn't even work."

"If it does, I can't wait to see his reaction when he communicates with Iggy for the first time."

"Me too."

Right on cue, Iggy came from around the sofa and jumped onto the seat in his wonderful costume. The face paint I would add right before we left.

Penny rushed over to Iggy and picked him up. "You are so cute!"

"I am, aren't I? Wait until I have my makeup on."

Penny looked over at me. "I have some green grease paint," I explained.

"You're really serious about this, aren't you?"

"I am. I'll have Iggy sneak close, see what everyone is up to, and then report back. That's it."

"That's it?" she asked.

"In theory. I'll play it by ear if there are any big surprises. My main issue is that if we are to be in stealth mode, I can't wear bright pink either."

Penny clamped a hand over her mouth, her eyes wide. "Don't tell me you're going to wear black?"

"I hate to do it, but what choice do I have? My blonde hair is more noticeable than Iggy's pink skin. I'll need to borrow something to cover it up."

"Don't you worry. I'll fix you right up. When I'm done, you'll be invisible."

"It will be an experience, for sure," I said.

"I'll run home, pick up a change of clothes, and drop Tommy off at Mom's. How about I come back at eight? That gives us an hour to get ready."

"Works for me."

I had to admit, I was rather excited for the adventure.

AT NINE SHARP, the three of us went downstairs to wait for Jaxson. It would be pitch black by the time we arrived at the forest, perfect for us not to be seen—or so I hoped. Even Penny and I had smeared some green face paint on to blend in better with the trees. I had to admit, we looked pretty good despite my totally black outfit. I just hoped some witch god in the sky didn't take away my powers seeing how I violated my rule of never wearing anything but pink.

"I am so excited," Iggy said as he popped his head out of my fanny pack.

I had to admit, he too looked good with his green face paint. Once in the forest, no one would see him. This plan was going to work.

Jaxson drove up, slipped out of the car, and looked right at us. "Glinda? You here?"

"You are funny." At least he hadn't said we could be seen a mile away. We got into the car. Naturally, Iggy jumped out of my pack that was situated on my stomach and onto Jaxson's chest.

He looked down. "You look amazing, dude."

"Thank you."

Jaxson stilled and then looked over at me. "What?" I asked as innocently as possible. I was sure with his heightened senses, he could hear my racing heart.

He looked back at Iggy. "Say something." Iggy opened his mouth and then closed it, saying nothing. "Darn. I thought I heard him talk."

Jaxson's disappointment hurt me. "Iggy. Be good."

He looked back at Jaxson. "Glinda put a spell on you so we can communicate."

"For real?" he said.

"For real."

Jaxson grinned. "That is so cool." He looked over at me. "Thank you!"

"I'm totally thrilled that it worked. I can't say how long it will last though."

"Any length of time is remarkable."

"Now that you are a semi-official witch, we should probably go." I didn't want to miss Hunter's lessons.

"Of course." He took off. After we passed through town, we arrived at the forest about fifteen minutes later. "Penny, did Hunter say where he holds these lessons?" he asked.

"Just that it was near his ranger station."

Jaxson pulled off to the side. "If we don't want to be seen, we should park here and walk in."

"I agree," I said.

We exited the car. We hadn't walked more than a hundred feet when Jaxson held up his hand. Without saying anything, he pointed in a direction different from what I was expecting. With his senses enhanced, I figured he heard Hunter or something.

"Take this." He handed me a flashlight.

I purposefully didn't have one because we'd be spotted in no time if I lit up the ground. "They'll see us for sure if I turn it on."

"It has a red filter."

I clicked it on. It illuminated the ground, but I bet unless we were close to my dad, we wouldn't be spotted right away. "Thank you."

Penny and I stayed together as we followed Jaxson. Iggy slipped out of my pack and crawled up my arm to sit on my shoulder. I'm guessing it was to avoid messing up his grease paint.

Because Penny and I were both wearing acrylic black

beanies, my blonde hair was tucked out of the way, giving Iggy free rein to roam.

"I remember this place," Iggy whispered.

"Shhh."

"Why should I be quiet? No one can hear me."

"How do you know there aren't other witches nearby?" I asked as softly as I could.

Jaxson turned around and placed a finger to his lips. Sheesh. He acted as if we were in enemy territory, and at the slightest sound, an army of soldiers would charge us. He might be right though. It was why I didn't want Iggy to talk.

In silence, we continued. After ten minutes, I touched Jaxson's shoulder and leaned close. "Are you sure we're going in the right direction?"

"I'm following the voices."

I couldn't argue with that. I leaned close to Iggy. "Do you hear voices?"

"Yes."

Okay then. Onward it was. Less than three minutes later, Jaxson stopped. He motioned me and Penny to look through the trees. "Someone is there," he whispered. "Turn off the light."

I did as he asked. I then moved next to him to see better. Oh, my goodness. Five men were standing in a circle. Too bad we weren't close enough to make out their faces. They didn't seem to need any light, which I found odd. True, the moon was full, but it wasn't as illuminating as a flashlight. Nor had they built a fire.

"Let me go in," Iggy said. "I'll eavesdrop."

I had asked him to come for this very purpose. I lifted him off my shoulder and set him on the ground. He scurried off, his feet sounding like a squirrel's, which meant his movements would not attract attention. In a few seconds, the darkness swallowed him up.

One of the men didn't seem particularly happy. I hoped they would stay put until Iggy was in position. We certainly didn't need them to find us—especially since I didn't think that Penny or I could outrun them. Sure, I had done a spell to make myself invisible, but since I hadn't memorized the words just yet, if I turned on my phone, the light would give away my position. Not only that, the best I'd been able to do was remain invisible for two minutes—hardly enough time for them to give up looking for me.

I strained to hear the conversation and hoped Iggy was learning why they were there. As I was trying to formulate a plan, the men grunted and then quickly divested themselves of their clothes.

Oh, no! Was this some sort of male ritual that I should not be witnessing? I closed my eyes. Then what sounded like bones cracking, followed by more groans split the air. I opened my eyes just in time to see all of the men drop to their knees and grunt in pain. I froze at the odd sight. What was going on?

Even though the dense trees blocked some of my view, it was obvious these men were changing—into wolves no less! Or had my imagination gone wild? It was a full moon, so maybe I'd just told myself to expect something like this.

My flight instinct kicked in, but as much as I wanted to get out of there, Iggy was somewhere in the forest. I couldn't leave him. I debated calling his name, but that would give away our position too.

Jaxson grabbed my shoulder and motioned me to get away from these animals—or rather from the men who had turned into wolves. My legs barely held me. "Iggy," was all I said.

Jaxson muttered something under his breath. "You go. I'll wait for him."

While I had faith that Iggy would do what Jaxson asked,

just then something crawled up my leg, and I almost screamed.

When Iggy's face came into view, I let out a huge breath and hugged him quickly. I spun around and took off. Penny was actually ahead of me, and Jaxson followed close behind.

I thought the wolves would follow us, but they must have been preoccupied. Given their special senses, they had to have smelled us.

The next ten minutes were the longest in my life. I didn't want to run full out for fear of tripping. Not only that, I was out of shape. And I wasn't ashamed to admit that I was scared—as in heart pumping, stomach churning type of scared.

I'd gone specifically to look for my dad and Hunter, but at the moment, I just wanted to reach the car, lock the doors, and take a deep breath. I wasn't mentally prepared for any more shocks.

When I spotted Jaxson's vehicle off to the side of the road, I almost cried. We all jumped in, and Jax started the engine.

"Is everyone okay?" he asked in a voice far calmer than mine.

"Define okay," I said. "Correct me if I'm wrong, but I saw five men change into wolves. I hope the rest of you did too." I crossed my fingers. It was a stupid superstition, but my brain wasn't functioning well right now.

"I saw them," Penny said.

"As did I," Jax chimed in.

Iggy hopped off my shoulder onto my pack. "That was so scary," he said. I wasn't buying it since Iggy was an animal, but I appreciated his sympathy.

"Tell me what happened," I said to my familiar.

"Before the men shifted, they were congratulating each other about the fact that Dirk Draper, who was the clan's leader, was dead. One of them was bragging that the cops believed Lou Owens was guilty thanks to their rehearsed story."

"Are you saying that Dirk and maybe Lou are, or rather were, members of some werewolf clan?" Jaxson asked.

"Yes," Iggy said.

"Did you recognize anyone?" he asked.

"No, but one man had his back to me."

Now that I knew that werewolves existed, it meant that my father, and maybe Hunter, could also be one. I couldn't become distracted with that right now as I certainly wasn't ready for that revelation. "What does everyone want to do?" I asked, hoping they didn't want to go back to the site or search for the others. If Penny insisted on finding Hunter, I'd have to give it a try.

"Go home," she said.

"Jax?" I asked.

"Let's get out of here. I think we've had enough of a shock for one night."

"Amen."

I don't think I could have gone back into the forest for any reason. I prayed my dad and Hunter weren't in there, even if it was to do some hunting. Those five wolves looked dangerous.

For the rest of the drive, we remained fairly silent. When Jaxson pulled in front of the Tiki Hut, I turned to both Penny and him. "What do we do now?"

"About the fact that werewolves exist?" Penny asked.

"Yes."

No one said anything. Oh, boy.

CHAPTER 13

To say I didn't sleep well last night would be an understatement. I wasn't a delusional person, which meant I wasn't prone to imagining things. I might have been able to talk myself into the idea that since I was under a lot stress lately that I had imagined seeing five men change into wolves. The problem was that Iggy, Jaxson, and Penny had seen the same thing. And that concept would have kept anyone up all night.

The big shame was that I hadn't gotten a real good look at the animal, but I was quite sure they weren't dogs. Their bodies were too big, and the shape of their faces were different from our domesticated canines.

I might have dismissed the whole idea had not Morgan Oliver, a ghost I met a few months back, said his uncle had been a werewolf. Even his aunt had more or less confirmed it. The fact my father just happened to leave for one or two evenings about the same time each month—during a full moon no less—made me believe he, too, could shift.

Only how was that possible? Something new must have

happened to him since this was a recent development—or so I wanted to believe.

If werewolf lore was to be believed, someone must have bitten him and turned him into one. That thought scared me more than anything, especially considering my father rarely left the mortuary. I shuddered to think someone broke into the house—one that was next door to where I lived—and attacked him. The fact my mother seemed completely oblivious was even stranger. I wouldn't be shocked though to learn she had been aware of it all and was play acting that nothing had happened in order to protect me.

Regardless of where this attack took place, it might explain why he had been weak for a while, and why I hadn't seen him. Perhaps when a person underwent the metamorphosis from man to wolf, it took a huge toll on the body.

But what did I know? The question now was what to do about it? I had a few options. One was to go back into the woods. Knowing Jaxson and Drake, they'd say it was too dangerous. Besides, what good would it do? No one would believe us anyway. I suppose I could talk directly to my dad about it, but that made me uncomfortable. He'd probably deny it, and I never would call him out as a liar.

My next choice was to drop this mess on the sheriff's department, and my last option was to ignore everything. That way I could go about my business of trying to figure out who had killed Dirk Draper and not be concerned about what my dad was up to.

Too bad Dirk was, in theory, the clan leader, who'd been murdered by one of his own kind. That meant finding the real killer was practically out of my reach since there was no way I could learn the identity of all of the members. Even if my father had been turned, I couldn't see him joining any kind of gang.

But letting unfinished business go was not in my DNA,

and since I avoided conflict at all costs, I should probably suck it up and tell Steve and Nash.

I'd fallen into bed last night without cleaning up, so before I did anything, I had to shower and then wash Iggy. I'd removed his *outfit* when we arrived home, but neither of us was in the mood to take off the grease paint—a process that would take some time. Besides, I think he liked being green for as long as possible.

Once I cleaned up and made sure my familiar was once more pink—ignoring his complaints along the way—I downed some breakfast while I mentally practiced what I was going to say to Witch's Cove's finest. Had I ever imagined I might have run into actual werewolves, I would have taken some video of the process. Considering it was night, I'm not sure how much the camera could have picked up, but the howls of pain during the transformation would have been heard for sure.

It wasn't too late to try to capture these men changing, however. I doubt Jaxson would agree to accompany me, but now that I knew where these men were located, I could go back tonight. The moon was still full, or mostly full, for the next two nights. I'd love to capture them on video changing from humans to animals. I wouldn't publish it, since that would be exploitive, but I would show it to Steve and Nash to let them know what the town was up against.

Most likely these shifters, if that was what they were called, wouldn't be discussing who killed Dirk Draper again tonight, which meant I'd leave Iggy home.

And yes, I was hearing the words, 'Too Stupid To Live,' in my head. I was smart enough to realize that if werewolves killed before, they probably wouldn't hesitate to do so again. Being stupid might apply to an ordinary person, but I had magic. I could become invisible.

That meant I'd have to spend the day memorizing the

spell so I wouldn't have to open my phone and have the light give away my position. I would still need it to video- tape them, but if I held my phone while I did the spell, the phone would disappear too. I'd tested that theory already.

I probably wouldn't need to be invisible for more than a minute, so I believed I could do this. I'd been practicing, and each time, my stamina improved. I would walk in, photo- graph the scene, and leave. By the time I reappeared, I'd be far enough away from them—assuming my scent didn't tip them off.

With that decision made, I headed to the sheriff's office to learn how they'd respond to this new threat. I could have waited until after I videoed the men, but if something went wrong, I wanted them to know who'd killed me.

To avoid being questioned by Aunt Fern, I slipped out the back entrance and then shot across the street. Pearl was at her desk, knitting. The moment she spotted me, she immedi- ately stuffed her needles and yarn in the desk drawer. Most likely, her grandson frowned on such behavior for a recep- tionist.

"Glinda! How nice to see you. Where have you been keeping yourself?"

As if she didn't know. "Keeping out of trouble." That was a big fat lie. "I would like to speak with the sheriff, if he's available."

"Of course." She picked up the phone and called him. Pearl disconnected and then nodded. "Go on back. Enjoy." She grinned.

I was certain Aunt Fern had mentioned that Jaxson and I were in business together, and as such, I wouldn't be inter- ested in dating Pearl's grandson. Okay, maybe it was more than just business. I liked Jaxson, but I wasn't ready to take it to the next level. Yet.

When I rushed past Nash to reach the sheriff's office, he looked up. "Glinda."

"Nash."

I didn't want to stop and chat, so I continued to Steve's office. I tapped on his door and entered before he had the chance to answer.

"Glinda, have a seat. Do you have news for me?"

He had told me to stop by if I learned anything about who might have killed Dirk Draper. I sat down in one of the two chairs in front of his desk. "I found out something, but I don't think you'll believe me."

"Oh?" As expected, his eyebrows rose. "Let me be the judge of that."

When the sheriff had investigated the murder of Frank Paxton, Steve was there when Frank's nephew told us about werewolves. True, this nephew was in his ghost form, but Steve seemed to take the werewolf announcement in stride. I had been skeptical that werewolves existed, but I no longer had any doubt.

I explained about my father leaving for a day or two at a time every month.

"What does this have to do with Dirk Draper's murder?"

"I'm getting to that. Because I wanted to see for myself if he really was learning to hunt with Hunter Ashwell, I went to the forest last night."

Steve's cheer disappeared. He held up a hand. "Let me get Nash in here."

I wanted to ask him why, but if he thought his deputy should hear my story, I wasn't about to complain. After a quick call, Nash came in, turned the chair next to me to the side and sat down to face me.

"You were in the woods late last night?" he asked. I caught a hint of fear in his voice and in his eyes.

"I was, along with Jaxson Harrison and Penny Carsted."

Iggy would be upset if I didn't mention him. "Iggy was there too. I dressed him in a camouflage outfit, complete with green face paint, and let him be our eyes and ears. No one would think twice about a small animal scurrying around."

"I imagine not," Nash said.

"Why did you have Penny with you?" Steve asked.

"She wondered if Hunter Ashwell, her new boyfriend, was a werewolf."

"A werewolf?" Nash's chin tucked under. "She really thinks he might be?"

I explained about the timing of things, and how the full moon seemed to play a role. "I thought my dad might be one, too."

Nash pressed his lips together. "Interesting. Tell me what you saw when you went into the forest."

I detailed how I'd put a spell on Jaxson to give him animal-like senses. "Both Jaxson and Iggy heard some men talking, so we followed the sound."

"What did you see?" Steve asked.

"At first, just men, so I sent Iggy in to eavesdrop."

Steve and Nash glanced at each other. "Then what happened?" Steve asked.

"All five men turned into werewolves."

Steve's eyes widened as his jaw dropped. "Are you sure that was what you saw? Did you shine flashlights on them or something to be sure?"

"No, but there was a full moon. The light bounced off their white skin. During their shift, they howled, as if they were in pain."

"Interesting. Go on," Steve said.

That was merely interesting? Not: Are you out of your freaking mind? His acceptance of my story confused me, but I continued. "Next time, I'll be sure to have my camera with me, so you'll have visual proof."

"Next time?" Nash asked.

I waved a hand. I wasn't sure I wanted to tell them I might take another look see tonight. "A figure of speech."

Steve leveled me with a stare. "Do. Not. Return."

Whoa. Did that mean he believed there were werewolves —ones who might be dangerous? "Why is that?"

I wanted him to tell me what he knew.

"I think it's obvious. Wolves are dangerous. Remember what they did to Frank Paxton. One of them tore the poor man apart."

"Morgan's twin brother claimed his other uncle killed Frank by shifting into a werewolf, but don't worry, I won't get caught."

The men looked at each other. "How can you be so sure?" Nash asked. "Wolves have an excellent sense of smell."

"I realize that. They might smell me, but they won't see me. Why, you might ask? I can become invisible."

I was sure they would ask for a demonstration, and I was ready—I think. If I froze under the pressure of these two watching, and I returned to the woods, how could I expect to succeed when it counted? I needed to do this demonstration.

"Invisible, you say?" Steve said with a high level of skepticism.

The idea of men changing into beasts seemed more acceptable to them than my ability to cloak myself. I lifted my chin. "Would you like a demonstration?"

"We'd love one," Steve said, amusement suddenly coloring his tone.

I pulled out my phone and tried not to let my hand shake. After I found the spell, I looked only at the screen. I didn't dare glance up at them for fear I would lose my concentration. With as much confidence as I could muster, I said the spell in a soft, soothing tone.

Their collective gasps made me realize I'd succeeded! Even the phone was nowhere to be seen. Score.

"Glinda?" Nash pushed back his chair.

"Where are you?" Steve said. "Well, I'll be."

I could have spoken, but I wanted them to be in awe a little bit longer. However, the longer I remained invisible, the more energy I would waste. While I couldn't appear on command, after practicing a few times, I found if I distracted myself, I could break the spell. I tried to read what was on Steve's computer screen, and bingo, I was visible once more.

"That was incredible," Steve said.

"Do you believe me now that I'm a witch?"

"I've believed you for a while, but I had no idea your talents extended this far," Steve said.

"I just learned how to do this, and even then, I can only hold the spell for a short period of time, because it takes a lot of energy."

"Then why do it?" Steve asked.

"Out of necessity? It's possible someone might come after me, and I'll need some kind of protection since I don't carry a gun."

"That's smart," Steve said.

Nash placed a hand on my arm to get my attention. "Glinda, I am impressed with your newfound ability. Thank you for showing us, but let me ask you this. Before the men shifted, did they say anything?"

I told them what Iggy said. Since I'd proven to Steve that Iggy and I could communicate, I hoped they believed me.

"Iggy heard one of the men say that Dirk Draper was their clan leader and that they were happy he was dead?" Nash asked.

"Yes, and that they are framing Lou Owens for it."

Nash whistled. "I wouldn't have guessed that."

"Me neither. I wasn't close enough, so I don't know who

was speaking. I asked Iggy if he recognized anyone, but he didn't." I held up a finger. "I should mention that one man had his back to my familiar, so that person could have been someone my familiar knew. Before you ask who Iggy has met, the only men related to the bowling league were Tinfoil Tim and Carl Edwards."

"Did the men say anything else?" Nash asked.

I had to say that Nash was being awfully accepting of my information, as well as believing that my pink iguana could relay information accurately.

"No. I might remember more later since I'm still shaken up. It was bad enough when I found out ghosts existed. In all honesty, that concept was easier to understand than werewolves."

Nash nodded. "Where exactly in the woods did you find these men?"

Did it really matter? "I don't know." I explained about letting Jaxson lead since he could hear and see better. "It seemed like we walked forever, but it was probably for only ten minutes."

"Thank you, Glinda. I appreciate you coming in," Steve said.

That was it? I'm not sure what I expected other than total denial on their part. So now what was I supposed to do?

It took all of three seconds to decide—I had to go back.

CHAPTER 14

I spent much of the day memorizing the few lines of the spell until I was certain I could do it. I disappeared a few times, but Gertrude was right. My energy was starting to wane.

"Are we going back to the woods again?" Iggy asked.

"Only I'm going."

He crawled up my leg. "Why?"

"I plan to take a video of them shifting, and that is all." Considering Steve and Nash seemed to believe werewolves existed, I'm not sure why I needed proof. Maybe I wanted to show Hunter and my dad that the woods were dangerous. If nothing else they needed to be cautious.

"What about your father and Hunter? Aren't you curious about them?"

I had to admit, my primary goal had been to figure out what was going on with them. Someone knocked on my door. From the sounds of it, it wasn't our esteemed sheriff's officers or Jaxson.

"Coming." I looked through the keyhole. It was Penny.

I pulled open the door to find her face tear-stained.

"Oh, Glinda. I did something bad." She rushed past me.

"Can I get you something to drink? Tea?"

"Yes, thank you."

I hustled into the kitchen, and she followed. I poured two glasses from a pitcher I kept in the fridge. I handed her a glass and then sat next to her at the two-seater kitchen table. "Tell me everything."

"I couldn't sleep last night, thinking about what happened."

"That made two of us."

She nodded in understanding. "From the few slips Hunter has made, I really believed he is a werewolf, possibly teaching other werewolves to shift."

My heart nearly stopped. "Are you saying, you believe my dad is one also?" It didn't matter that I suspected it too.

"Maybe."

"What happened to make you so upset?" I asked.

"I confronted Hunter."

I whistled. The girl had more guts than I did. "Did he admit to being this human to animal shifter?"

"Not at first. When I told him that I had talents too—namely that I could detect a lie—he relented."

I wanted to make sure I understood this. "Hunter told you in no uncertain terms that he's a werewolf?"

"Yes."

Not that I didn't believe my best friend, but sometimes she could get things wrong. It was possible that Hunter told her what she wanted to hear. "Did you tell him you saw the werewolves last night?"

"Yes."

"How did he react?"

"He was very interested," she said.

There was that word again. "Why is that?"

"He wouldn't tell me."

"Did Hunter say if my father was one too?"

She shook her head. "Our conversation didn't get that far. I was talking to him on the phone when he said he had to go."

That seemed bogus. I guess the big question was whether Hunter, and maybe my dad, were part of this group of men who laughed about killing their leader and then didn't seem to have any qualms about framing an innocent man.

"What are you going to do?" I asked.

She reached out and cupped my hand. "I was hoping you'd be willing to find Hunter with me. Tonight. In the woods."

That had been my plan, but I worried about having Penny with me. She might run up to Hunter. For all I knew, he would shift if he feared exposure and then become a danger to others. Yikes. "How about if just Jaxson, Iggy, and I go?"

"You don't trust me?"

The hurt in her eyes tore at my soul. "I trust you, but we don't know how Hunter might react. It could break the two of you apart." I was grasping at straws.

"If I don't see for myself, how can I trust him?"

She was right. "Okay, let me see if Jaxson is willing to go with us."

"He'll say no way. He'll worry we'll run into those original five men. They are dangerous as humans, let alone wolves. Jaxson won't let you go in, even if he is by your side."

I probably should suggest we table the whole thing until next month, but these clan members needed to be held accountable. My mind shot to the werewolf, Charles Paxton, who had killed his brother, Frank. Frank owned a necklace to keep him from shifting. Charles Paxton was in jail, not for the killing, but for stealing the magical necklace.

I wondered what happened to him on the first full moon? Did everyone in that prison now know about werewolves?

Not knowing these answers was driving me crazy. "If that

is the case, Iggy and I will do this—alone. I'll take my camera and cloak myself. I'll then videotape it all. We can show it to you."

Penny pressed her lips together. "That plan is dangerous. What if you can't hold your invisibility shield?"

That was a major concern. I could continue to practice, but that would only lessen my chances of succeeding tonight. I blew out an exasperated breath. "Why can't things be simple? But if only Hunter and my father are there, they won't harm me."

"And if there are others?"

"You have a point."

Penny's eyes sparkled. "I could speak with Hunter again and ask him if your father is a shifter. Would that work? I mean, do you really want to see him take off his clothes and shift? The shifting process seems really painful. I know you, it would tear you apart to see your dad like that."

"It will be terrible and terrifying, but my dad needs to know that I'm okay with it. I want him to trust me with his secret."

"At least tell Jaxson," she pleaded.

"I will, but he might lock me in a room so I can't go at all. I suppose Steve and Nash might investigate, but they are more vulnerable since their hearing and eyesight aren't as good as Jaxson's. They might go in with guns blazing."

"Why don't you think about it for a while," Penny said. "I'll see if I can come up with a workable plan. We wouldn't be leaving until nine, right?"

We? I thought I would be going alone. "Yes."

"Are you going to talk with your dad this afternoon to judge his frame of mind?"

"I would, but I worry I'll give something away." I pushed back my chair, leaned over Penny and hugged her. "It'll be okay."

She huffed out a laugh. "I can't believe you're using our standard phrase."

"It's all I got, girlfriend."

Once Penny left, I went to the living room and dropped onto the sofa to think. Naturally, Iggy had been eavesdropping. He hopped up next to me. "I think we should go."

"If I had one of those Go-Pro cameras, I could strap it on you and let you record everything."

Iggy's tail went crazy. "Yes. Please?"

"No." Though at some point, The Pink Iguana Sleuths might have to invest in one. "I'm torn. If I thought those Clan members would leak some information about Dirk's death again, I'd try to find them. Once more, I've practically dumped the killer into the laps of the sheriff and his deputy. Even if they were able to round up all five men, they'd deny everything. We need real proof."

"Didn't you say you and Jaxson were going to speak with Lou Owens? He should be warned that men are trying to frame him."

"Yes, but the hard part will be telling him how I know." I stood. "Thanks, Iggy."

"For what?"

"For suggesting that Jaxson and I warn Lou that he is being framed."

I could debate this ad nauseam with Iggy, but he didn't have the analytical mind that Jaxson did. I grabbed my keys and phone and headed over to the wine shop. I figured Jaxson would either be working for his brother, or be upstairs on his laptop, digging up some dirt on someone.

I entered through the bottom floor, but I didn't see him. Drake was alone in front. "Hey, stranger," I said, trying to sound upbeat.

"Glinda! Jaxson told me about your adventure last night."

I wouldn't have used that word. "More like a nightmare."

He nodded. "I thought he might have been pulling my leg, but from your expression, he wasn't."

"No. I need to speak with him. Is Jax upstairs?"

"Yes."

"We will catch up soon, okay?"

Drake smiled. "I'd like that. Maybe another ice cream sundae night."

Just hearing those words brought down my blood pressure. "It's a date."

I rushed upstairs to find Jaxson at the white board. "Figure anything out?" I asked as I studied the board. He'd crossed out quite a few names, including Lou Owens. "I'm assuming you're narrowing down the list to potential werewolves?"

"Yes, and since none of the people in the circle last night were women, it's safe to eliminate them."

"Do you have any reason to believe they are members of our bowling league?"

"No."

That was what I was afraid of. "So now what?"

"You tell me."

"I say we speak with Lou Owens and warn him," I said.

"Warn him of what? That a bunch of werewolves claimed they were trying to frame him for Dirk's death?"

I didn't see what was wrong with that strategy. "Why not?"

"If Lou is not a werewolf, he'll laugh in our faces. The last thing we need is Lou telling everyone in Witch's Cove that the new sleuths in town are some crazy people."

Darn. "If he is a werewolf, we might be able to get him to tell us who else is one."

Jaxson set the marker on the tray, faced me, and lifted my chin. "I love your innocence, but it ain't happening."

I stepped back. "Why not?"

"Because he'd be a dead man by the end of the day if he gave away that list."

It was probably the same as any gang. "Then what about talking to Charles Paxton?"

"The werewolf who killed his own brother and stole one of the magic necklaces? Being an upstanding member of the community, I'm sure he'll tell us."

Sarcasm did not become him. "You think other members would find out and kill him?"

"Yes," Jaxson said.

"What if we bribed him with one of the necklaces? He wants it."

Jaxson escorted me to the other side of the panel and guided me to the sofa. "You could promise him freedom from prosecution for the rest of his life, and he wouldn't tell you anything."

"Then what are we to do? Even if we could lasso the five men and drag them to the station, we can't prove anything."

Jaxson shrugged. "I guess if they remained in the cells until the next full moon and then shifted, it would prove something."

"But not who killed Diamond Dirk."

Jaxson crossed his arms and leaned back. "We're not going back and taking pictures, if that is what you're thinking."

I could play this game. "Why not?"

"It won't prove who killed Dirk."

Something was bothering me. "How about if we tell Lou Owens about someone wanting to frame him, and then we follow him? Don't you think he'd go to the source?"

"You mean to his clan and ask around?"

"Precisely."

Jaxson tilted his head to the right and then to the left. "I suppose it could work."

My pulse soared. "Iggy can cloak himself, like I can, though I don't know how long he can last. Even if he appears, I doubt anyone would try to kill him. They won't know he can talk."

"Assuming you paint him again."

"I can cover his whole body. No one will recognize him as my pink familiar." I was beginning to like this idea.

"Before we step one foot into the forest, we have to lay the groundwork by telling Lou the truth about him being framed."

"We won't mention werewolves or our little spy. How about if we say we were taking a moonlight stroll in the woods looking for a campsite for the night when we came across five men. We heard them laughing over something." I laid out the rest of my plan.

Jaxson leaned over and kissed my forehead. "You, Glinda Goodall, are a genius."

"I am?"

Jaxson laughed. "Let's do this."

CHAPTER 15

Jaxson and I had talked about letting Steve and Nash in on our intended interaction with Lou Owen, but then we thought better of it. They would just tell us not to interfere. It was their job to follow Lou—not ours. While true, they still didn't possess any magical abilities, and they might end up being attacked by these wolves.

Taking all of these factors into consideration, we decided this called for some Witch's Cove magic. Hence, mum was the word.

"I found out that Lou gets off work at three, which means he's probably home now," Jaxson said.

"It would be difficult to speak with him if his wife is there. He might not be as open about things if she is listening."

"I agree. Here's what we'll do," Jaxson said. "We'll go to the house. If Lucy is there, we'll tell her we've changed our minds about the house for now, but if we decide to move in together, she'll be the first to know."

I loved having a second opinion. "I like it. It gives us flexibility, though I suspect she'll think it a bit odd that a client would show up at her house."

"Hey, it's Witch's Cove. People are friendly, right?" He smiled, and I immediately gave in.

"You're right."

Jaxson picked up a piece of paper and waved it. "And I have the address."

"Let's go."

With the directions in hand, we drove out to Lanky Lou Owens' house. No cars were in the driveway, but it was possible their vehicles were parked in the garage.

"Ready?" Jaxson asked as he cut the engine.

"I hope so." I rang the bell and was pleased that Lucy's husband answered.

"Yes?" Since we'd never met, he'd have no idea who we were.

"Is your wife home?" I asked. His answer would dictate which story we went with.

"No, I'm sorry."

Story number two. "I'm Glinda Goodall, and this is my partner, Jaxson Harrison. We have some information about the death of Dirk Draper that we feel you should be aware of."

"Dirk's death? Do you know who killed him?" he asked, his hand gripping the door frame.

"Not yet. May we come in. We won't be but a minute."

"Ah, sure." He escorted us inside. His home was neat and well appointed, but it wasn't grand. The lack of pretense implied he might be approachable.

"Have a seat," he said.

Jaxson and I sat next to each other on the sofa. "Jax and I were hiking last night, planning on finding a good campsite, when we came across five men who were, shall we say, a bit rowdy."

"Oh?"

I waited a beat to see if he would say anything about the dangers of being in the woods on a full moon, but he didn't. "Since we didn't want to disturb their little party, we waited before passing through. While we were there, we overheard one of the men bragging about killing Dirk Draper and then framing you for the murder."

His jaw tightened. "What?"

I thought I'd made myself clear. "We didn't hear much else, but it was something about you believing your wife was cheating with Dirk and that you wanted to get back at him. I'd have to assume they told the police this information."

Jaxson placed a hand on mine. "I didn't feel it was safe to be around murderers, so we turned around and came back home."

Lou dragged a hand down his jaw. "I can't believe this," acting as if he hadn't heard a word Jaxson had said.

"I'm really sorry." I meant it too. "We thought you should know. I'm not sure what you can do, unless you know who these men are."

His gaze shot to my face so fast, I almost jerked. "No, I don't, but I intend to find out. Thank you for telling me."

Jaxson stood, and I followed suit. "By the way, we just joined the bowling league. Thursday was our first time there. Lucy said you were ill, which is why we haven't met before, and it's why we came to warn you." That didn't make a lot of sense, but my nerves made me babble.

"Oh, yes. The bowling league. Thank you."

My creep meter was growing, so Jaxson and I hurried out. Step one of the mission accomplished. We hopped into the car and took off. Instead of returning to town, Jaxson parked close to the intersection of Lou's gated community and the main road. If Lou left, we'd see him and then follow.

Forty-minutes later, we decided he wasn't going after

anyone—at least not right away. "Either he has no idea who these men are who framed him, or he knows they are were-wolves, and he plans to go after them tonight," I said.

"I have to agree." Jaxson started the engine and headed back to town.

To say I was a little disappointed would be an understate-ment, but if we followed the man tonight, we might see the wolves shift again, assuming Lou knew who had killed Dirk. For that, I would take a video.

We decided to stop at the Spellbound Diner for some-thing to eat, so I would be ready for our big adventure. If I had to disappear for whatever reason, I'd need my strength. Dolly wasn't there, but that was okay. I really only wanted a meal.

We sat in a booth in the back, and I had to admit, it felt good to be in familiar surroundings.

A young girl approached. "What can I get for you?" she asked with her pad in hand.

I ordered a hamburger and a sweet tea, and Jaxson wanted the baked fish and a coffee. As soon as she left, I turned to him.

"How do you propose we follow him? If we assume he's going to the woods, I guess we could wait for him inside the forest entrance, or should we park outside of his house and follow him from there?" There were pros and cons to both scenarios.

"It's still a full moon, so the men should be in the forest since they need to shift."

As would my father.

Before we could discuss our plan further, Pearl Dillsmith walked in and looked around. "Oh, lookie. Pearl's here."

I waved and smiled. When she caught sight of us, she made her way over to us. "Glinda and Jaxson. How nice to see you two."

She'd just seen me. "Would you like to join us? We just ordered." I scooted over in the booth.

"Don't mind if I do."

Instead of sitting next to me, she motioned for Jaxson to slide over. He swallowed a smile and obliged. "It's so awful about that real estate man," Pearl said.

Good. She'd come here looking to gossip. Most likely she'd wanted to chat with her pal, Dolly, who didn't seem to be here.

"I know. I heard someone is trying to frame Lou Owens for it." This was what I had told Steve and Nash, so I figured she already knew.

"Yes, it is a terrible thing."

"I'm thinking it might have been Tinfoil Tim—or rather Tim Bowers." That wasn't true, but I wanted her to spill the beans.

"Not Tim. Right after he finished bowling, I heard he went into the woods."

I sucked in a breath. "No! Are you sure?"

I wasn't sure how that was relevant, because if he was in the woods at the time of death, how could he have been killing Dirk? However, the woods implied he could be a werewolf too. Did they congregate when the moon wasn't quite full too? I really needed to read up on my werewolf lore. Though, after what I saw, there was no lore about it. It was real.

"Yes. His associate confirmed it."

"His associate? Who is that?" I wondered if it was Produce Polly. She was on his team and a good bowler.

"Daisy Carson."

"Who?" I'd never heard of this woman.

"A fellow believer in aliens," Pearl said.

This was getting weirder by the minute. "Where exactly did Tim say he was at the time of the murder?"

"I told you. In the woods."

"Why was he in the woods?" Pearl was not a good story teller.

"A friend of Tim's called him as he was leaving the bowling alley. She said she spotted a spaceship hovering over Hendrian Forest."

"That's a scary thought," I said.

"I agree. Tim wanted to make contact with them, so he drove out there," Pearl said.

"Why would he do that?" Jaxson asked. "If he wears a tinfoil hat, puts aluminum foil on his house windows, and claims to have been abducted, shouldn't he want to stay away from all things alien?"

Pearl's mouth opened slightly. "I don't know, but that makes sense to me, unless he wanted to do them harm or tell them to not bother him again."

Yeah, that would work. Not. "What did Steve think about his story?"

"He didn't believe him, though I think he is trying to get a reading off the GPS in his car to see where he went that night."

"That is smart. Did this friend confirm Tim's story?" I asked.

"I don't know."

"Why would the sheriff think Tim might have wanted to kill Diamond Dirk?" Jaxson asked.

"In theory, Tim really liked Lucy."

That was a new one. "Tim and Lucy? Really?" I held up a hand. "I don't know Lucy very well, but she seems like a professional woman who is well put together, as my mother would always say, while Tim is...unorthodox."

"I'm just telling you what I hear."

That was the definition of hearsay. "I see."

That gave Tim about five reasons to want Dirk dead, but

that didn't mean he did it. I personally hadn't seen any tinfoil hats on any of the men who'd shifted into wolves.

The waitress stopped by and took Pearl's order. She only asked for coffee, which implied she'd come to see Dolly. I'm surprised the two hadn't memorized each other's schedules.

Once the food arrived, I avoided any discussion of our plans for spying on Lou Owens. I didn't want that information to reach Steve or Nash.

"Fern tells me your office is almost finished," Pearl said in between sips of coffee.

"Yes. I just need some curtains and a few knick-knacks, and we'll be done." I looked over at Jaxson to see his reaction to that fact. He took a final bite of his fish and nodded. He was such a guy.

"Have you had many clients?" Pearl asked.

For a moment I thought perhaps Steve was employing his grandmother to spy on us, but I quickly dismissed that thought. He wouldn't stoop that low, or would he? If I were him, I would so use her to find out things. "Not yet, but I haven't advertised."

"Oh, I see. I'm sure Steve will send some clients your way if he doesn't have time to deal with a case."

Most would consider that a castoff, but I would call it a paying customer. "I think The Pink Iguana Sleuths will cater to a different kind of clientele than those who would seek out the law."

She smiled. "I understand. Will you be doing spells for people?"

"Spells?" I nearly spit out my tea. "Like a love spell or something?"

"Why not? Or someone wants a second opinion on how their loved one died."

I had anticipated that request. What they did with my discovery was up to them. "It's possible."

"Or they may want you to speak with their loved ones directly."

"That's my mom's thing."

"Not unless a ghost is present." She smiled.

She was referring to my ability to speak with Morgan Oliver, the nephew of Floyd Paxton. "Maybe."

Jaxson finished his meal and placed his napkin next to his plate, a sign he was ready to go. I too had finished, while Pearl was nursing her coffee. To my delight, Dolly came out from the back. When she spotted us, she hustled over.

"Pearl, I am sorry I wasn't here. I had to take care of something."

Pearl slipped out of the booth and turned to us. "Nice chatting with you both."

Apparently, we were merely a nice diversion. "You too."

Since we would be working late tonight, I thought the company should pay for our meal, which meant me. Once I paid, we returned to the car, which Jaxson drove about five hundred feet to the Wine and Cheese Emporium's small parking lot. "I'm not sure what else we can do until later tonight," Jaxson said.

That was a hint that he wanted a break, and I couldn't blame him. "At nine then?"

"How about eight thirty? I want to be there for when Lou arrives. Would you mind if we take your car?" he asked. "He might recognize mine."

"Sure. I'll pick you up at eight-thirty."

He smiled. "But I'm driving."

A girl could get a complex. "Sure thing, but what do I tell Penny?"

"The truth?"

"That might work."

CHAPTER 16

"Maybe he's not coming," I said. Normally, I was a patient person, but not when it came to something my dad might be involved in. "I'm glad Penny's not here. She'd be a mess."

Before I had the chance to call Penny, she'd contacted me to say she had no one to watch Tommy. I promised we would update her with any news.

Jaxson leaned back against the inside car door. "Stop fretting. He'll be here. You saw the look on Lou's face. He plans to confront these men."

"What if they shift and kill him?"

"I'm guessing he's also a werewolf," Jaxson said.

"Even so, it would be five against one."

Jaxson opened his mouth to respond when a car pulled down the road. We ducked, and I actually giggled—nerves most likely.

"What's so funny?" Iggy asked.

I didn't answer until I was sure the car had driven past. "Nothing."

"Let's go," Jaxson said.

With my black beanie concealing my hair, I grabbed Iggy and my phone. This time, I didn't take any flashlight. Jaxson had dressed all in black and had somehow found black face paint, making him almost invisible. It was kind of creepy.

My spell to enhance his eyesight and hearing appeared to be intact. I had tried my spell of invisibility one time today to make sure I could recite it without using any help, and I had succeeded.

I grabbed Jaxson's arm to make sure I didn't trip, in part because he was taking very long strides. Without holding on to something, I'd be flat on my face in no time.

The car stopped a few hundred feet past the entrance gate. A man parked and got out. It was Lou. I would recognize that lanky frame anywhere. To my shock, he stripped, tossed his clothes in the car, and then shifted into a wolf. My breath left my body, so much so that I had to tighten my hold on Jaxson's arm.

"Glinda, snap out of it," Iggy said as he dragged his nails lightly down my face. It was enough to bring much needed air back into my body.

"I'm good." Or so I wanted to believe.

"Let me know if you need me to slow down," Jaxson said, as he took off at a trot.

Seriously? I raced after him. I understood his need to hurry. He was chasing a wolf. Lou had disappeared deep into the woods, and eventually I couldn't even hear any leaves rustling. From the way Jaxson was charging forward, he was following the man's scent or maybe the sound of his footsteps. I figured, even if I lost sight of him, Iggy would guide me.

I had to give Jaxson credit. He would often look behind to make certain he could still see me. I couldn't say how long we traveled, but eventually we slowed.

A soft light shone through the trees, and Jaxson stopped. He motioned me near. "This is as far as we go," he said.

The clan had lit a fire. How nice of them, but we weren't nearly close enough to hear much. I wanted to move in but understood that wouldn't be smart. Instead, I set Iggy on the forest floor, all dressed in his cute camouflaged outfit. He took off, clearly understanding his role.

A howl sounded—and not a friendly one. The men's chatter stopped as a wolf emerged from behind a bush. One of the men in the group held up his hand. "Lou," he said.

These might have been the same five men from before. The show was about to begin. With my phone in hand, I placed it against my chest to prevent the light from accidentally showing. "Sum como montinero..." I whispered. When Jaxson looked over at me, I finished the spell silently.

Holding my breath, I looked down and saw nothing. I'd done it! I darted from tree to tree, trying to make as little noise as I could. Just because I was invisible to the human eye, it was possible a werewolf could see me. Fingers crossed he couldn't.

I stopped, looked down at my phone, and pressed video. I then held it out, hoping to pick up something. Whoa. The wolf growled, snarled, and then shifted into a human. It was Lou, whose naked body was thankfully obscured by the bush.

"Carl, Bill, Doug, Tom, and Eddy. I heard an ugly rumor."

My heart fluttered. This was it. He'd actually said the names of the men.

"What rumor, Lou?" The voice sounded familiar. He'd called one of them Carl. Could that be Carl Edwards, the bowling lane manager? I really needed him to turn around.

"That one of you killed Dirk."

"You heard right," said the man with his back to me.

I had to get a better look. Not having any idea how long I could hold this cloaking, I moved a few feet to the right.

When the man with his back to me turned to the side, I froze. It was Carl Edwards. Wow. I looked down at my camera. The lighting was terrible and grainy. I tapped the screen to set the focus and aperture, and it helped—but only a little.

"Why?" Lou asked.

I'd have to thank him later. I wanted to know, too.

"Dirk thought he could prance into our clan from Canada, throw some money around, and take over. You of all people know how hard that was for all of us. You were supposed to be the Alpha after Charles was incarcerated."

Charles? Holy moly. Were they speaking about Floyd Paxton's brother? The same brother who killed Floyd for the necklace that could prevent him from shifting?

I pushed aside that thought and listened. If I didn't concentrate, I'd appear, and not even Jaxson would be able to save me.

"I was, but I had no intention of killing him over it."

"Now you can lead," Carl said.

"Maybe. I heard another rumor," Lou said.

"What's that?"

"That someone among you was trying to frame me for the murder. I'm guessing with me out of the way, you, Carl, would be the Alpha."

I sucked in a breath, and I swear the sound echoed for miles. Lou looked around. "Someone's here. I smell another wolf."

Oh, no. It was time to leave. Wait a minute. They smelled another wolf? That wouldn't be me. It didn't matter. I didn't need to be close to some kind of clan war.

I wanted to call out for Iggy, but I couldn't afford for anyone to hear me. I hoped that my familiar was aware of my presence and would follow me.

The problem was that as I headed back the way I came, my arms and legs turned weak. My vision blurred. Fearing I might drop my phone, I quickly shut it off and stuff it in my pocket. Whatever video I had recorded had to be enough to prove that the bowling alley manager had killed Dirk Draper and then framed Lou.

I searched the woods for Jaxson, but I couldn't find any landmarks. Shouts sounded behind me, forcing me to move faster. Were they coming after me? I ran. And then I tripped, my face slamming against the ground.

"GLINDA, CAN YOU HEAR ME?"

I heard something, but I didn't know who was talking to me. All I remember was falling and experiencing a lot of pain and weakness. I tried to open my eyes, but they wouldn't cooperate.

Something lightweight crawled up my arm. Iggy! Had he asked me the question? If I didn't open my eyes, I'd never know. With a great deal of effort, I lifted my lids. Except for a dim lamp, the room was dark.

"Hey," someone said.

"Jaxson?" I looked around. I was in a room, but it wasn't one I recognized. "Where am I?"

"Take it easy. You had quite a fall. You're at my house."

"Your house?" Now I was the one to repeat someone else's comment.

"Yes."

I pushed up on my elbows, trying to ignore the pounding in my head. I lifted my hand and tapped my forehead that was bandaged. "What happened?"

Jaxson turned up the lamp to a brighter setting. I squinted. "All I know is that you did your spell, disappeared, and then charged toward the men. I could see a few things in the woods but not a lot. A wolf approached who shifted into Lou."

"Yes. He asked who had killed Dirk."

"Who did?"

"You couldn't hear them?" I asked. He did have super hearing.

"Only bits and pieces. We were pretty far back, and the forest was noisy."

"True. To answer your question, it was Carl, the manager."

"Carl is a werewolf?"

I don't know why he was so surprised. It seemed there was a whole other species living right under our noses. "So, it seems." I told him what I'd heard. "Then the men stopped talking because one of them said there was another wolf present. I heard a growl and figured it was time for me to get out of there."

"I'm glad you did."

"How did I get here? All I remember is tripping and falling."

Jaxson picked up Iggy, who crawled onto his shoulder. My heart swelled. "This little guy came and got me. Naturally, I followed, since the men who'd all turned into wolves had taken off. You'd wandered in the wrong direction of where I was waiting."

"I am so sorry." I told him about feeling weak and disoriented.

"Glinda, didn't Gertrude warn you that might happen?"

"In a way, yes, but I figured it weakened her more because she's old."

Jaxson picked up my hand. "I think you should consider giving up this invisibility thing. It's too dangerous."

He might be right. "Maybe spying while invisible isn't the best use of my talent."

"No." Jaxson stood. "Rest. It's late."

"Wait." I slipped my hand in my pocket. "I want to see how much of the conversation I caught on video."

"Glinda, rest. You have a concussion on top of the magic doing a number on you."

He sounded like my mother. "I want to look." Unfortunately, when I pressed the button to turn on the phone, it didn't come on. "Seriously?"

Jaxson slipped it from my fingers. "I bet it ran out of juice. I'll charge it while you sleep."

I wanted to complain, but I didn't have the energy. "I want Iggy to stay here."

Jaxson smiled and set him down. "Iggy, take care of her."

"You got it, boss."

Boss? It didn't matter. I was thrilled that the two of them were getting along.

As much as I wanted to assemble all of the puzzle pieces, my brain was too tired, and I gave in to the comfort of the bed.

CHAPTER 17

Sunlight streamed in the window, forcing me to roll over. I didn't want to get up, but someone was wide awake. Iggy crawled up my back, over my shoulder, and then hopped in front of me. I didn't open my eyes. "I'm not getting up just yet," I told Iggy.

"You have to. We have a killer to catch."

A killer. "Didn't we already solve the crime?" Or had I imagined everything?

"We both know who did it, but we have to convince Steve to arrest Carl," he said.

Carl? The scene unfolded in my brain. "I need coffee."

I opened my eyes and eased to a sitting position, ignoring the pounding in my head. So this was Jaxson's house. I think he said he was renting it, and that it had come with furniture, but I wasn't sure of anything. I had been surprised to learn he wasn't living with Drake, though I suppose working for his brother—before I came onto the scene—and living with him, might have been a bit too much.

"Move," I told Iggy. I didn't want to squish him. "We both need to clean up."

"I like being green."

"I'm sure you do. The sheets, however, may never be the same." There was grease paint all over the pillows and the sheets. I guess I'd be buying Jaxson a new set.

I sat up and then exited the room. I figured there had to be a bathroom close by. I located it, and then washed my face, hands, and arms. It was the best I could do without taking a shower. I studied my face in the mirror. I looked like a wolf had attacked me. I was dirty and slightly bloody. I peeled off a bandage, pleased the gash was superficial.

When I had repaired the damage the best I could, I followed my nose and found the kitchen. Iggy was already on the counter, acting as if he lived there. "Iggy, get down."

Jaxson smiled. "It's okay. He's free to roam wherever he wants."

"Thank you."

Jaxson motioned to the small table. "Sit. I made you coffee and some scrambled eggs. It won't compare to Miriam's brews, but it will have to do."

He was the sweetest man. "I had no idea you could cook."

"You'd be surprised at all the skills you can pick up in prison."

Ouch. Someday, I'd ask him what it was really like to be in there—especially when he knew he didn't belong. I sat down, eyeing the steaming mug he'd placed on the table. "Were you able to charge my phone?"

"I was. I thought we could watch it together." He carried over my plate of scrambled eggs. My stomach grumbled, and I dug in.

"This is really good."

"I'm glad you like it."

Without being invited, Iggy joined us. I turned on the phone and found the video. Jaxson pulled up a chair, and together we watched. Would it win any cinematography award? No, but I could make out most of the men's faces. All that really mattered was that Carl confessed to killing Dirk. Except for when Lou stepped forward, the bush mostly blocked my view of him.

Then someone said something about hearing another wolf. That was when the men started to shift, and then I took off. After that, I remembered nothing. "Where were you?" I asked Jaxson.

"I climbed a tree. I was banking on them not being able to. It seems as if they were more interested in finding that rogue wolf."

I sipped my coffee and gobbled down the eggs. I hadn't realized how hungry I was. "Thank you again for saving me. Did you carry me back to the car?"

"Like a fireman."

No wonder my stomach was sore.

"I led him to you," Iggy said with a lifted chest.

I petted him on the head. "Yes, you were a hero, too."

"Are you planning on showing this video to Steve?" Jaxson asked. "I know you said he and Nash seemed to believe you had seen a man shift, but this is proof."

"I have to show him. He might be able to do a little editing that shows the part where Carl confesses. I don't think a court of law is ready to learn werewolves exist."

"I agree. How about I drive you home, so you can clean up, and then we'll head over to the sheriff's office?"

"That sounds great. And don't worry about the messed-up sheets. I'll buy you a new set."

He placed his hand on mine. "I got this, sweetheart."

There was that word again. Jaxson said it so casually that I was sure he called all the girls that, but I liked it, none-theless.

"YOU READY TO DO THIS?" Jaxson asked as we walked across the street to the sheriff's office.

"I'm here, aren't I?"

"You are."

Pearl's eyes widened when we walked in. "This is a surprise."

I'm not sure why she would say that, but I needed to focus on the task at hand and not chat with her. No telling what I would spill. "We'd like to speak with Steve and Nash."

"Sure. I'll let them know you are here."

Before we were halfway to the back, both of them came out of the sheriff's office. "Glinda. Jaxson."

I waved my phone. "I have proof that Carl Edwards killed Dirk Draper," I said rather softly unsure if I wanted Pearl to hear.

"Really? Let's sit in the conference room. It's sound proof."

That was good. Steve nodded to my phone. "Is that your proof?"

"Yes."

"I'm guessing you went against my strict orders not to approach these dangerous men—men who you claim can turn into werewolves."

"They did change, and I have proof."

Not that I didn't trust Steve, but I emailed myself the video just in case he decided to confiscate or delete it.

"Tell me."

I explained that no one should be falsely accused of a crime, and Lou was about to be railroaded into being called a killer.

"I would never let that happen," Steve said. "Without proof."

"Good to know. Anyway, since we bowl in the same league, Jaxson and I spoke to him. I told him that Jaxson and I had been looking for a place to camp for the night when we came across five men. They were laughing about killing a man, and about framing him."

"I assume Lou Owens was stunned?"

"Yes, and then he was angry. I figured he knew who these men were and would confront them."

"You should have let us handle this," Nash said.

"I didn't want you two getting killed."

Steve huffed out a laugh. "Why would they kill us and not you?"

"Because I have magic on my side. I can shield myself. Remember?"

"There is that," Steve said. "Go on."

"I think the video will explain it all." I showed it to them on my small screen.

Both Nash and Steve watched with extreme interest. "It's hard to make out everything," Nash said.

"True, but you can see Carl's face. And it's clear at the end that these men at least start to change into wolves. Once they heard another wolf, I ran."

"Good. As wonderful as this video is, I don't think the courts would believe it's real."

"Because Lou shifts into a man?" I asked.

"Yes."

I sat there for a moment, trying to think of a way to prove Carl was guilty without the video. "Can either of you think of a reason why Carl would kill Dirk? Even if he was a bad leader, can't they dethrone him or something?"

Nash seemed to hide a smile. "I'm not sure it works that way in a clan."

How would he know? "I believe in the lion kingdom, if another male lion comes in, he challenges the leader to a fight to the death. Smashing someone over the head with a bowling ball is cowardly."

"I agree," Nash said.

I snapped my fingers. "Carl told me that he played a game with Dirk after the league ended, and that Dirk bowled at least a few frames after that. Maybe you could look at the scoreboard to see if he told the truth." I assumed everything was computerized and imagined the scores would be kept in some kind of database.

Steve pulled out a yellow pad from his desk drawer and made a note. "That's a good idea. We're still trying to find the murder weapon."

"Carl has a ton of photos in his office of him with his tournament ball," Jaxson said. "I noticed he'd used more than one, but the ball he used most often was green. Find his stash of balls and check it for hair and blood, and the man will go down."

"We checked every ball at the alley, but we came up empty. I'll see about getting a warrant for Carl's home." Steve pushed back his chair.

At least the killer hadn't used my pink ball. I wanted to tell them that if they needed help with handling the were-wolves, they could ask Hunter Ashwell, but it wasn't my place to tell them that their forest ranger was one.

"I'm not sure Lou will cooperate, but if he is willing to talk to you, he might be able to confirm what I said. He should have an insight as to why Dirk died and who was involved," I said.

"We plan to contact him, but I really need both of you to stay out of it from here on out. I don't care if you can become invisible or not, it's too dangerous."

"It's more dangerous for Lou. If I were Carl, and I'd

confessed to killing Dirk and framing Lou, I'm thinking someone might decide the other needs to go." Thinking about that concept, churned my stomach.

"We agree," Nash said. "It's why we plan to go out there again tonight to make sure it doesn't happen."

"You think you can stop five or six wolves? If you kill them all, animal control will be all over you."

"Don't worry about us. We have it under control."

What did that mean?

CHAPTER 18

After we left the sheriff's office, I was a bit depressed. "It's over, isn't it?" I asked Jaxson, even though my question was rhetorical.

"Seems to be. We learned who killed Dirk Draper and gave the sheriff enough evidence to clear your name."

I looked over at him. "You know I never believed Steve thought I was guilty, right?"

He smiled. "I know, but it gave you a good excuse to investigate."

I huffed out a laugh. "True. Now that this is over, I need to move on. I should take Iggy's advice and come up with a marketing plan to drum up business."

"I think helping to solve this case will be the leg-up we need. The gossip queens, and then the other bowling team members will get the word out for us that we were instrumental in taking down Carl Edwards."

I hoped that was true. "What can they say though? We recorded men admitting to the murder—men who then turned into wolves? They'll think we're crazy."

He shrugged. "Maybe, but I trust Steve will put a positive

spin on it." We walked across the street. "What are your plans now?" he asked.

"I am going to pick out some material for the office curtains. Aunt Fern said she'd make them for us."

"Pink curtains I'm guessing?" One brow rose.

Since we were partners, I probably should ask if he was okay with that. "Do you see any other color?"

"Are you kidding? I'm all into this pink stuff now." Jaxson turned to the side, slid his fingers under his jeans, and pulled up his briefs—make that his pink briefs.

I clamped a hand over my mouth to keep from shrieking. "You have pink underwear! Whatever possessed you to buy those?"

He pretended to look crestfallen. "You don't like them? You liked my pink wrist band, my pink socks, and my pink T-shirt."

I laughed. "I do love them. And thank you for embracing the pink."

"Anytime, sweetheart." He winked. "Have fun shopping."

He saluted and headed off toward the Cheese and Wine Emporium, while I went to my car. Once on the road, a bit of euphoria surfaced. I'd helped solve another crime. Today would be about simple things, like picking out fabrics, and perhaps organizing a little party for my parents and friends to see our new space.

Because Jaxson was being such a good sport by wearing pink, I ended up going with pink and navy-blue striped curtains instead of solid pink. It was a nice blend of boldness and my fetish for pink. I'd already measured the windows, so it was a matter of buying the material and then finding the hardware for the curtain rods.

An hour or two later, I returned with my stash. Aunt Fern was working at the checkout desk. When she finished her shift, I would give her my purchases.

"How did the big reveal go?" Iggy asked just as I walked in the door. He lifted his head rather defiantly.

Yes, he was a bit peeved that I didn't let him come with us to the sheriff's department, but it wasn't as if anyone could understand him anyway—other than myself and Jaxson. "I told them the important role you played in everything."

"You did?"

"Yes."

He hopped up and down. "How did they react to seeing men shifting into animals?"

"With not as much disbelief as I would have expected."

"Why is that?" Iggy asked.

"I don't know."

"What's next?" He sounded quite excited.

"I don't know that either."

He planted his stomach on the ground. "Oh."

For the first time in what seemed like forever, I had nothing to do. The case was finished, and we had no potential clients knocking on our door. Even though it was in the middle of the day, I decided to grab my e-reader and head on over to Maude's tea shop. I deserved a sweet tea and a spot of food.

"If Aunt Fern stops by, can you give her the curtain material?" I asked Iggy.

"I guess."

He always got that way after we wrapped things up, but I couldn't do anything about it. "You can visit Aimee. Tell her whatever you want."

He blinked few times. "I like that idea."

With renewed energy, Iggy dove through the cat door while I left by the side entrance and walked over to Maude's shop.

I picked out a jicama and cream cheese sandwich on a

sourdough roll, as well as ordered a new blend of tea. I'd just sat down when Jaxson rushed into the shop.

"I've been looking for you," he said as he pulled out the chair across from me.

"Why didn't you just call?"

"I think you forgot to turn on your phone."

"No way." I checked it, and sure enough I had. "Sorry. What's happened?"

He leaned forward. "Carl Edwards is dead."

I was too stunned to respond at first. "When?"

"Apparently, last night. When the sheriff and Nash went over to his house with the search warrant for his bowling ball, they found him—or so says Dolly."

Thank goodness, the gossip queens were hard at work, though why Aunt Fern hadn't heard I don't know. "How did he die?"

Blood coursed through my system. I was turning into a crime junkie, in need of the next mystery to solve.

"His throat was ripped out."

I inhaled. "Don't tell me by a wolf."

"Dolly said that Pearl had to hang up before she could give her all of the details."

I did adore those two women. "Did either of them know who might have done it?"

I was sure that Jaxson, as well as the Steve and Nash, were thinking it was a member of Carl's clan. My guess would be Lou Owens.

"Lou Owens."

Nailed it. I thought about it for a moment. "It makes sense. Carl basically threw Lou under the bus regarding Dirk's murder."

"True. I suspect Steve and Nash will question Lou, but I doubt he'll let on that he knows anything."

"Most likely. I wonder if Lucy has any idea why all of this is happening?"

"I can't imagine she would marry Lou and be unaware he was a werewolf," Jaxson said.

"My dad is probably one, and he didn't tell Mom—or at least she's never mentioned she knows. I imagine that would be a difficult conversation to have with me."

"True."

Maude came over wearing a smile. "Jaxson. Nice to see you again. What can I get you?"

"I'll have a coffee and that sandwich Glinda is having."

"Coming right up."

Not wanting anyone to hear, I leaned forward. "Do you think women can be werewolves?"

He chuckled. "I don't see why not. I would think the clan would become extinct rather quickly without them."

"That might be true in the real wolf clan, but not necessarily in the shifter world. It's possible only men can actually shift."

"I wish I knew."

Speculating would do no good. "Who besides Lou would benefit from Carl's death?"

Jaxson reached across the table and cupped my hand. "I normally wouldn't say this, but considering these are dangerous animals, we probably should back off on this one and let Steve and Nash handle the investigation."

Darn male logic. "I know you're right, but it goes against my nature to do nothing."

Jaxson leaned back in his seat and shook his head, clearly frustrated with me. "What do you think you could do? And do not say you'll become invisible and sit in Lou's house waiting for him to call a friend and confess."

When he put it that way, it sounded ridiculous and

dangerous. "As much as I don't want to admit it, I don't have this invisibility thing under control."

"You think?"

I chuckled. "For now, at least."

"Glinda, you could have died. I may not be there the next time."

My blood pressure dropped. "Okay. I get it. What do you suggest we do?" I sipped my tea.

"Like I said. Let the law take care of this. Let's give Steve and Nash a few days to sort things out, and then we'll confront them about their progress. What if this clan learns we were involved in leaking the information to Lou about the fact that Carl framed him?"

My blood ran cold. "They'd kill us, too."

"Exactly. Can we agree that the best thing to do is nothing?"

"Yes, but I'm still going to work the grapevine."

He lifted my hands. "Your nails look too good to go in again."

"True, but I could use some produce."

"What will Produce Polly know? Honestly, you should speak with Hunter. He's already admitted to Penny that he's a...you know what. And, he works in the forest. I wouldn't be surprised if he's aware of the clan."

The lightbulb went on. "That's it. You're a genius."

Maude delivered Jaxson's order. "What are you two chatting about?"

Darn it. I should give her something, though I wouldn't be surprised if she'd already heard the news. Dolly knew. "The manager of the bowling alley was found dead in his home this morning."

She sucked in a breath. "Oh, no. Tell me what you know."

Yeah, that wasn't going to happen. "That's all I know."

"Then why is Jaxson a genius?"

"He...ah...suggested I speak with some of the captains of our bowling league. They might know who'd want to do him in."

"That is smart, Jaxson. If you learn anything, be sure to pass on the information. Remember, gossip flows both ways." Maude winked and left.

In relative silence, we ate our meal. "Ready to see what Hunter knows?" he asked.

"Absolutely." I totally believed that Hunter was not a member of this clan. If he was, then we'd be in serious trouble.

The trip to the forest was a little nerve wracking. The whole time I was trying to figure out how to approach the topic of Hunter and his werewolf alter ego. Even if he was aware of this evil clan running around the forest, Hunter might not want to divulge that he knew. I also didn't want to put his relationship with Penny in jeopardy.

Once we parked, we located the station that was home to a small museum. Inside, the walls had images of trees with the names of each species underneath. There was also a section for the different animals one might find in the forest.

A woman was manning the desk. Next to her was a pamphlet stand filled with hikes one could take, as well as literature on the area. "Can I help you?" she asked.

"We would like to speak with Hunter Ashwell. Is he here?"

"He is on his rounds."

Darn. I supposed we could wait, but it could be hours before he returned. "Do you have his number?"

"What is this about?"

"His girlfriend, Penny." Darn it. Why was my go-to mode always a lie?

The receptionist's eyes widened. "Is she okay?"

"Yes, but I'd like to speak to him. I'm Penny's best friend."

"Oh, I see." She pulled out a piece of paper and wrote down his number.

"Thank you."

We stepped outside. "What are you going to ask him?" Jaxson asked.

"I'm going to start by telling him the truth."

"Good idea."

I called Hunter. Before he could say much, I launched into the spiel about how Jaxson and I had videotaped some men shifting into wolves. "Penny told me you were one."

"I am."

His quick admission surprised me. "Another werewolf was murdered last night."

"Who?" His concern sounded genuine.

"Carl Edwards, the manager of Pinarama."

"You thinks he's a werewolf?"

"Yes," I said. "I have a video of him shifting."

Hunter said nothing for a minute. "I think we need to talk."

Yes! "I'd like that." I explained that we were already in the Hendrian Forest in front of what I assumed was his office.

"Wait there. I'll be there shortly."

My hand was shaking when I finally hung up. "He's on his way."

CHAPTER 19

Hunter pulled up in a Jeep, parked, and then motioned us inside. "Let's step into my office."

He nodded to the woman at the desk and continued toward the back. Once inside, he closed the door. "I hope I can count on you two to keep quiet what I'm about to reveal," Hunter said.

"Of course," Jaxson said before I had the chance.

Hunter looked right at me. "Glinda? I need your promise that you won't be spreading the word to anyone—and that includes Penny."

I swallowed, not sure I wanted to know. "That's asking a lot."

"I know, but if I didn't think your life could be in jeopardy, I wouldn't say anything now."

My stomach nearly revolted. "Someone wants to harm me?"

"Possibly. Let me start from the beginning. I'm hoping when I give you a little bit of background information, you'll understand."

Jaxson reached over and grabbed my hand. His warm, firm grip helped calm me. "I'm listening," I said.

"I have confessed to Penny about my identity. I care a great deal for her and wanted to make sure my werewolf side wouldn't be an issue between us. Had she not been a witch, I probably wouldn't have let things progress this far."

When he stopped talking, I figured he wanted me to respond. "She cares a lot for you, too."

"That's good to hear. You should know that Nash and I go way back."

Nash and Hunter? Jaxson squeezed my hand and then let go. "Is he also a werewolf?" Jaxson asked.

"He is."

Oh, boy. I really wanted to ask about my father, but I didn't think I was ready to hear the truth. "Go on."

"We both lived near the Canadian border where many werewolf clans exist. It's how we met. Some of the clans are benevolent and others are not."

"I take it the group that Dirk Draper belonged too was not one of the good ones."

"You catch on quickly," Hunter said. "Nash and I, along with a few others, were hired by a group of high-ranking werewolf leaders to learn the habits of these less than savory kinds and identify where they lived. It became clear rather quickly that this one particular clan was out for blood—specifically human blood."

Chills raced down my spine. I couldn't comprehend any of this. "Why?"

"It's the nature of the beast, I suppose. Some people are born bad, others not. Dirk Draper was one of the unscrupulous ones. As a werewolf, he was even worse."

I tried to connect the dots. "Did you follow Dirk down here?"

"I did. Our plan was for me to establish myself here and

learn who else was a clan member. When Floyd Paxton was murdered by one of the members, I contacted Nash. I knew at that point I needed help."

Had Nash been happy to get the call or upset? "What would he have done if there hadn't been an opening in the Witch's Cove sheriff's department?"

"Nash is very talented. He could easily have been my assistant, but we figured there would have been some sheriff's department who could use a highly decorated officer. As soon as I thought I might need him, he studied to become an officer in Florida."

That explained a lot. I could see now why Nash kept his background so secretive. "How much does the sheriff know about you two?" I asked.

"Everything. These wolves can be very dangerous, and Steve needed to be aware of them."

"Did Steve ask for proof? The sheriff likes certainty."

Hunter smiled briefly. "You'll have to ask him—or Nash—but let's say it took some persuading on Nash's part to convince Steve that our kind exists."

I could only imagine what that entailed. For now, I'd let it go.

"Why would Dirk come to Florida from Canada?" Jaxson asked. "Besides for the more favorable weather."

Hunter leaned back in his seat. "About that." He held out his hand. "See this ring?"

"Yes. It's nice. Is it your college ring?" It had a garnet stone.

"It says the name of my college, but it's a special ring, one that is imbued with magic."

My mind shot back to the garnet necklaces that Floyd Paxton had. "Don't tell me this keeps you from shifting on the full moon."

He nodded. "Yes. Both Nash and I have one. However, no

one in the Athabascan Clan possesses one—that's the clan that Dirk and Lou ran here."

"Athabascan?"

"That's the region where some of the original wolves hailed from."

"Oh. If these men don't have your type of ring, it means they are forced to shift on the full moon whether they want to or not, right?"

"Yes, though apparently, one of their members, Charles Paxton, had procured a magic necklace, but I believe you know all about that."

My vision blurred for a moment. "Yes."

Both were now in a safety deposit box in the bank that only Steve had access to.

"The reason Dirk specifically came here was because he believed there were witches in or near Witch's Cove who could help make more magic rings. I believe all werewolves —good and bad—want the cure so they can have more control over their lives."

I could understand that need. "If they didn't have to shift on the full moon, does that mean they might not be so violent—if that is the word?"

"That's hard to say. I think these men want control over every aspect of their lives, including the ability to kill without prosecution."

"Because the world doesn't believe these man-changing beasts exist."

"Exactly," Hunter said.

"If you and Nash have these rings, why didn't Dirk and his fellow clan members stay near Montana and have the witches there help?"

His brows rose. Apparently, I had impressed him. "We're not originally from Montana."

"Oh." When he didn't say where he was from, I figured he

didn't want me to know, and that was fine by me. "You said that I might be in danger. What did you mean? I might be a witch, but I'm not a very good one. Most people around here know that. I doubt I could put a spell on jewelry to prevent men from changing."

"That may be, but I don't think the Athabascan's realize that. After all, you ended up with two magic necklaces. They have no idea if you were the one to imbue the stone with power or if it was someone else."

I clasped the pink stone that hung around my neck. It held my magic source. It was possible someone learned I could determine how a person died. "It wasn't me."

"Glinda, you have to admit that you have been pretty visible in the community of late," Hunter said.

"Are you saying that because I've been helping Steve that I became a target?"

"Yes. It's why we believe your dad was also targeted."

"Targeted?" I grabbed the edge of my seat to keep from falling off my chair. "What are you saying?" My throat was so dry, I had a hard time saying those words.

"I wouldn't have said anything, but Penny told me that you've suspected for a while now that your dad's a werewolf."

"She has," Jaxson said. He must have sensed that I was struggling to put the words in order.

"I'm guessing one of Dirk's clan members bit him?" I asked.

"Again, this is speculation on our part, but we believe they were going to use him as leverage. Since your father needs the cure, the clan probably figured that you could be convinced to provide it for everyone."

I huffed out a laugh. "That's ridiculous. I couldn't do a spell like that. Look at Iggy. He's still pink, despite my recent attempts to change his color."

Hunter wove his fingers together. "To a non-witch, all witches do spells; there is no limit to their talents."

"That's plain wrong. I'll tell them I can't help them." Assuming I even wanted to.

Hunter shook his head. "I'm not sure they'll believe you. When I overheard what these people had done to your dad, I stepped in and offered to help him."

"Help him how?" I asked.

"As a human, he would have no idea what to expect. I wanted to make his transition easier. We made up the story about him taking hunting lessons."

It all fell into place. "I see."

"The first few times your dad shifted, it exhausted him. It's not easy, but with practice, it becomes less painful."

I sank back into my seat. "That's why he was weak and pale."

"Yes. As much as the idea was abhorrent to him, during the time when he was a werewolf, I helped him locate an animal to eat. That completed the cycle. From here on out, he will be fine."

"My mom said that my father has super human strength."

Hunter smiled. "I'm not sure about super human, but our hearing and eyesight are exceptional, and our strength is superior to most."

"Is that why you can throw a bowling ball so hard?"

He chuckled. "No, my father was on the pro circuit. I learned at a young age how to bowl. I don't play much because I don't want to lose focus about what is important. My father's life was bowling almost to the exclusion of his family."

"I hear you." I had a tendency to have tunnel vision myself. I needed to learn that lesson.

"Does my dad know that I suspect he's a werewolf?"

"He knows I plan to tell you—for your safety."

"And my mother?"

"He told her recently. Your dad feels terrible this has happened. He didn't tell you only because he didn't want you to worry."

I huffed. "You mean he feared I'd rush out and try to find these evil werewolves." In truth, it is what I did.

Hunter's smile was brief. "Yes."

We were back to that topic. "What can I do to let the clan know that I can't help them?"

"If I knew, I'd tell you. Right now, they are probably more worried about who is going to be their leader than how you can help them. From what I've been able to piece together, after their Alpha was murdered, Lou Owens was to be their next leader. Then their third in command, Carl Edwards, decided to frame Lou. I can only guess he wanted to be in charge."

I whistled. "It's dangerous to be a clan member."

"No kidding. In theory, Lou is in charge, but Steve and Nash are investigating whether or not Lou killed Carl. If so, he'll be imprisoned."

"If Carl had done that to me, I would try to take him out," Jaxson said. "The man admitted to framing Lou."

"That doesn't excuse murder—if Lou killed Carl."

"If Lou is found guilty, how can he be in jail though? Won't he shift on the next full moon?"

"Yes, which is why our kind always manages to have those prisoners escorted to a more secure facility—one that is for werewolves and run by werewolves."

I whistled. "I had no idea. Who is next in line after Lou, now that Carl is dead?"

"That I don't know. I wish we had an inside man, but we don't. That being said, even if I had a photo of every man, I wouldn't know the pecking order. We can't charge them with being in a clan, because no court would believe these men can transform into wild animals."

"They do have the perfect cover," I said.

"They do. Their biggest threat seems to come from within their own ranks."

I looked over at Jaxson and then back at Hunter. "There is nothing we can do to help?"

"Let Steve and Nash do their job. They'll find out who killed Carl."

"I'm more concerned about what we can do to keep Glinda safe," Jaxson said.

Hunter pressed his lips together. "How about asking Steve for one of those necklaces to give to her dad? If he no longer has to shift, the clan can't use him as leverage."

"I love the idea, but Frank Paxton was killed because of the necklace," I reminded him.

Hunter nodded. "Perhaps he can use the necklace for a few days and then return it to the bank vault—with Steve as his bodyguard."

"That certainly is a possibility."

Someone knocked on Hunter's door. It was the lady who manned the desk. "Someone needs your help, Hunter," she said.

I pushed back my chair. "I can't tell you how much I appreciate your honesty. And I'm doubly happy for Penny. I hope things work out between you two."

Hunter smiled. "So do I."

CHAPTER 20

As soon as Jaxson and I returned to town after speaking with Hunter, I called Steve to find out about Carl's death. Normally, I wouldn't have asked, but now that I had all this inside information about what was going on with the werewolves and such, I thought I could be an asset.

"Nash and I have collected the evidence from the crime scene and have sent it off to be processed. We're waiting for the results."

That was all? "Are you going to arrest Lou?"

"Glinda," Steve said. I knew that tone.

"What?"

"We will question all of those who might have wanted to harm Carl. And yes, Lou is at the top of our list, but I haven't decided if I want to tip him off that we suspect him of murdering Carl. I want to wait until I get the test results back from the bowling ball to see if Carl killed Dirk first."

"Suppose you learn Carl did murder Dirk, how does that affect your decision to arrest Lou?"

"I have my reasons. Now can you please let me do my job?" Steve asked. "And stay out of it. Wolves are dangerous."

"Okay, okay. I won't do anything, but the suspense is killing me. Hunter thinks a wolf or two might be targeting me, because I have magic."

"Yes, I know. We have discussed it, which is why you need to keep a low profile."

Low profile, indeed. That was like asking me not to breathe. "I promise I will not go anywhere near the Hendrian Forest, nor will I speak with Lou Owens. Happy?"

"Very. Thank you."

I disconnected, not at all satisfied with the discussion.

"What did he say?" Jaxson asked.

I relayed the message. "Which means Carl's death is off the table for now."

"Then perhaps now would be a good time to work on our marketing plan."

"I suppose it has to be done at some point." Even though my mind would not be on it.

THE NEXT TWO days were hard. Really hard. I wasn't built to wait for test results. While I understood the need to advertise and promote our new company, I wanted to do something regarding Carl's death. Before I tackled that, however, it was time to talk to my parents, mostly to assure them that I would help in any way I could. I'm sure having to tiptoe around me couldn't have been easy for either of them.

I went next door and found my father in his study. "Knock, knock," I said as I entered.

Dad looked up. "Glinda."

I didn't like the way his lips were pressed firmly together. Clearly, he was dreading this talk as much as I was. "I'm so sorry I kind of got you into this mess."

"Hunter told you?"

"Yes."

"You had nothing to do with my...*condition*."

I sat in the chair across from him. "It's because of me that you were targeted. Hunter told me that because I had found the garnet necklace, which prevented a werewolf from shifting, that this Athabascan Clan of wolves thinks I can put a spell on a ring or necklace for them."

"Really?"

Ugh. Hunter must have told my father all of this already. "Yes, really. These clan members are desperate for a solution to their full moon shifting. They thought if you were afflicted that I would help put a spell on rings for them—like the kind Hunter has." I didn't mention Nash since I wasn't certain his identity was common knowledge.

My father stood and opened his arms. "Come here, sweetie."

I couldn't remember the last time my father asked for a hug, but I wasn't going to turn down the chance for an embrace. I stood and stepped into his arms and hugged him. "We'll figure this out."

"I know we will."

For the next few minutes, I detailed how he could borrow the garnet necklace so that he didn't shift. "I suggest you stay inside for that time."

"Trust me, I will." He sniffled, and his relief made me want to cry too.

"How is mom holding up?"

He sighed. "She's mad that I didn't come to her right away. She knew I'd been bitten, but I truly thought it had been a wolf. Only after I started to feel strange on that first full moon that I sought the help of the forest ranger. I had no idea Hunter was a werewolf."

"I'm glad you had someone."

Mom peeked her head in the den. "You two okay?"

"Yes. Dad and I were just discussing the strategy for him dealing with the full moon."

Mom looked over at my father. "I bet you're relieved that Glinda knows."

"I am."

The three of us talked out what I'd learned. "Right now, I'm letting Steve and Nash find out who killed Carl Edwards."

"I'm glad you're keeping out of it," Mom said.

"I am." More or less. I was serious about not going into the forest or speaking with Lou, but there was nothing wrong with asking my trusty gossipers a few questions.

Once I finished visiting with my parents, I returned to the office. Jaxson was at his desk working rather intently. "I'm going to grab a bite to eat at Dolly's diner." Talking to my parents gave me an appetite. "Want to come?"

He looked up. "You're going to gossip or eat?"

I couldn't fool him. Ever. "Both?"

Jaxson closed his laptop. "Then yes. I'm coming with you. I'm hungry."

"Good. I just had that dreaded talk with my father."

"I want to hear how it went."

On our walk over, I told him everything. "It was actually nice. I haven't felt that close to my dad in a long time."

Jaxson smiled. "I'm really glad."

"Me too."

We entered the Spellbound Diner. Thankfully, at two, the place was mostly empty. Dolly looked up, smiled, and waved.

I waved back.

"What are you hoping to learn here?" Jaxson asked. "The case is practically closed."

"You never know what Dolly has learned in the last two

days. The death of Carl Edwards will be all the town is talking about."

"Are you convinced Lou is the killer?" Jaxson asked as we slipped into a booth.

"For now, I am, but I'm always open. He does have the best motive."

I picked up the menu. As much as I wanted something decadent, I would function better on a meal not laced with sugar.

Dolly came over. "Do you know what you want?"

"I do." I ordered the grilled cheese and a sweet tea. Jaxson asked for the meatloaf and a cup of coffee. "If you have a minute, can we pick your brain?" I asked.

"I thought you'd never ask." Dolly grinned and then rushed back to the counter.

I leaned back. "Do you think we should tell Lucy that we aren't interested in a home anymore? I don't want her to spend time looking when we aren't serious."

"I think that would be nice," Jaxson said. "But I would suggest a phone call. She might be able to see the lie in your eyes if you tell her in person."

I opened my mouth. "Are you saying I'm a bad liar?"

He laughed. "Sweetheart, I can always tell when you're fibbing."

I could never fool him or Penny. Before we could continue the discussion, Dolly slid in next to Jaxson and across from me. "Is this about Carl's death? Do you know who killed him?"

She got straight to the point, didn't she? It was why I often came here first. "Unfortunately, we know nothing at this point. It seems as if Steve is focusing on proving that Carl killed Dirk and not on who killed Carl. I think he wants to close that case before opening another one."

"Smart. I do have a bit of news though." Her eyes lit up

light like the Fourth of July. "About an hour ago, Lucy came into the diner with someone looking to buy a house."

"Makes sense. She is a realtor." I'm betting Lucy would have learned that Carl had been murdered. "How did she seem?"

"Like nothing had happened. I heard her mention to this person about the sheriff questioning Lou regarding his whereabouts on the night of the murder. Lucy was totally disgusted that anyone would think her husband was capable of killing anyone."

"She might be prejudiced," I said.

"True, but first the sheriff thought Lou killed Dirk, and now he suspects Lou may have killed Carl."

"Steve has to question everyone." Besides, I thought the same thing. "What did Lucy say about Carl's death?"

"Lou was supposedly with friends at a pub about five miles from town the night Carl was killed."

"Good intel. I'm assuming Steve checked Lou's alibi?" I asked, my voice trailing off. I couldn't believe Lou was with friends. I was so sure he was guilty. Or were his friends covering for him?

"I'm assuming he did, but you'd have to ask him. People do lie, that's all I'm saying." Dolly leaned closer. "There was something strange about Lucy today."

My pulse shot up. "What was it?"

"She had bandages on both of her arms, as well as a small scratch at the base of her neck. When I asked her about it, she said one of her neighbor's dogs attacked her."

"Whoa. That's terrible. I've never had a dog, but I wonder if she provoked the animal. Why else would he attack?"

Dolly shrugged. "I didn't want to ask too many questions and embarrass her in front of a potential client."

"That was smart."

Someone behind the counter called Dolly's name. "Gotta go. Let me know if you find out anything."

"Sure."

Dolly rushed back to the counter. "What are your thoughts on Lou and Lucy?" I asked Jaxson. "If Lou really does have an alibi, who's left?"

"Anyone else in the clan. Maybe the guy next in line, whoever that is."

That meant I could no longer be of any use. Darn. "I wonder if the medical examiner can tell if a female wolf or a male wolf attacked the victim."

His eyes widened. "I suppose if she tested the DNA. Are you thinking maybe Lucy killed Carl?"

"Why not? Assuming she's a werewolf. Think about it. Carl sets up her husband to take the fall. Maybe Lou is letting bygones be bygones, but Lucy can't let it drop. Though it's always possible, since Lou is now in command, he ordered someone to assassinate Carl."

"That would make it hard to pin the murder on Lou. On the other hand, Lucy could sneak into Carl's house and kill him," he said. "She might have gone over pretending she wanted a truce or something."

"It would explain the marks on her arms if Carl shifted. He might have wanted to warn her but not kill her. I'm wondering if the medical examiner will test to see if there is blood under Carl's fingernails."

"Probably not if she is assuming his attacker was a real wolf."

One of the servers delivered our meal. On the first bite, I groaned, not realizing how hungry I really was. Jaxson seemed equally famished.

"If Hunter told us the truth about everyone's alter ego, maybe they told Dr. Sanchez about the existence of our furry friends," Jaxson said.

"If these forest dwellers plan on staying around, more people could be killed, which means Dr. Sanchez needs to know what she's looking at when Steve delivers a body."

"After we eat, do you want to plead your case to Steve and Nash about bringing Dr. Sanchez into the inner circle—assuming she's not already?"

I smiled. "I love that we think alike."

We finished eating, paid, and then headed across the street to the sheriff's office where Pearl was devouring a plate of cookies. She smiled with a mouthful and held up a finger. A moment later, she swallowed. "Steve isn't here, but Nash is," Pearl said as a way of a greeting.

"Nash will do."

"Go on back."

Nash watched us approach. "Can we talk in private?" I whispered.

"Sure." He stood and we followed him into Steve's office. "I thought you told Steve you wouldn't investigate," Nash said.

"I'm not." Actually, I only promised not to enter the forest or speak with Lou Owens.

He took the seat behind Steve's desk while we sat in front. "Okay. Spill."

"According to Dolly, the owner of the Spellbound Diner, Lucy Owens was in this morning with bandages on both arms. She also has a cut on her neck."

He appeared to be trying to figure out the significance of that. "Are you suggesting she might have been in some kind of altercation with an animal?"

"Yes. Jaxson and I thought you could maybe ask the medical examiner to test under Carl's nails to see if he had any defensive wounds. A wolf did attack him."

Nash laughed. "And you think maybe that wolf is Lucy Owens?"

My stomach cramped at his incredulity. "Are you saying she's not a werewolf?"

"I wasn't the one to question her, so I don't know if she is or isn't. But she might be."

Jaxson leaned forward. "Does Dr. Sanchez know about the existence of werewolves?"

"No."

"Don't you think it's time she did? I realize that her findings might not hold up in a court of law, but at least you'll know if you should be looking for a human."

Nash leaned back in his seat. "I will definitely bring that up with Steve. Personally, I agree with you."

I hadn't expected that. "Good to know."

He smiled. "Any other tidbit of gossip you'd like to share?"

His tone was a bit condescending, but I couldn't blame him. Other than the video I took of the men changing into wolves or, in the case of Lou, from a wolf into a man, I usually came in with hearsay and hunches.

I pushed back my chair and stood. "No. And good luck."

"Thank you."

We left the sheriff's office. "I'm surprised you didn't press Nash for more information," Jaxson said.

I smiled. "That's because I have an idea."

He dipped his chin. "Glinda."

"Don't get your pink briefs in a wad." I then laughed.

CHAPTER 21

"I don't think this is wise," Jaxson said as he pulled down the street from Carl Edwards' house and parked.

"You aren't thinking Mrs. Edwards might have killed her husband, are you?"

"No, but she might be a werewolf herself and not take kindly to questions."

I looked over at him and smiled. "Then I guess you'll have to earn your keep as my muscle man."

He chuckled.

I wasn't sure what I would say to the grieving widow, but I usually was pretty good when I had to think on my feet.

A woman with rather red eyes answered the door. "Yes?"

"Mrs. Edwards?" She nodded. "I'm Glinda Goodall, and this is my partner Jaxson Harrison. We bowl at Pinarama. Your husband will be missed."

"Did you know Carl well?"

"We only met him recently."

"Where are my manners? Would you like to come in? You'll have to excuse the mess."

Score! "Thank you."

She wasn't kidding about the mess. Sheets covered a sofa and a chair. I would guess this was where the attack took place.

"The dining room is about the only place that hasn't been disturbed."

It also might cause fewer memories to surface. "Jaxson and I run The Pink Iguana Sleuths. We're friends with many in the league and want to help bring the criminal to justice. The sheriff seems more focused on other aspects of the case." I thought that was relatively accurate.

"I believe I know who killed my husband."

For some reason, my mouth just opened. "Was it Lou Owens?"

Her eyes widened. I knew it. "No."

"Really? Then who?" I asked, rather stunned.

"His wife— his cheating wife."

Being a female, Lucy had not been near the top of my list until I learned of her bandages. "Were you here when your husband was murdered?"

"You mean when he was attacked by that wolf woman?"

"Yes."

She glanced down at her hands. "No, I was at my sister's. My nephew is ill, and I was helping her out."

"Why do you suspect Lucy Owens, Mrs. Edwards?" Jaxson asked.

"Why? Because she was involved with my husband. When I found out, I told him either she had to go, or I would leave him." Mrs. Edwards wrung her hands together. "I'm the one with the money, you see. That's why I knew Carl would make the right choice. He had to cut off the affair."

I had to take a moment to think this through. "You believe that when your husband basically dumped her, she killed him?"

"Yes."

I didn't buy it. I glanced at Jaxson, and from the slight tilt of his head, he wasn't buying it either—not that Lucy didn't kill Carl, but the reason behind it. "Did you know that Carl was upset with the order of the clan leaders?"

Her cheeks reddened. "You know about that? But you're not..."

"No, Mrs. Edwards, we are not, but we hear things."

"I don't pay much attention to Carl and his men, but I do know that no one liked Dirk Draper. Good riddance to him."

I wasn't going to ask if she thought her husband had anything to do with his death. She'd probably deny it. I really wanted to ask her if she was aware who would become second in command—assuming Lou wasn't arrested—but I figured Steve could deal with that too. I stood. "Thank you for taking the time to speak with us. Again, I am sorry for your loss."

She sniffled. "If you're really sorry, you can make sure that hussy pays for what she did."

Jaxson stood too. Only then did it occur to me. "May I ask you one more question?"

She looked up. "Sure."

"Do you have any evidence that Lucy and your husband were involved?"

"Why, yes I do. They communicated on some app on their phone. He called her Miss Lucky, and she called him Ravenous Man. Silly really."

Her name at the bowling alley was Lucky Lucy. It fit. "Do you have your husband's phone?"

"I do."

I wanted to be the one to deliver the final clue to Steve and Nash, but that might ruin what relationship we had. "Do you think you could show the phone to the sheriff? He'd be very interested in hearing your thoughts on who murdered your husband."

"If you believe it will help. I can barely believe Carl is gone. The more I think about it, the more convinced I am that Lucy Owens killed him though."

All of this was supposition then. The phone might focus Steve's investigation in Lucy's direction though. "Thank you."

We let ourselves out. Once in the car, Jaxson turned to me. "You continually amaze me."

His words made my face flush. "Why?"

"Mrs. Edwards' belief that Lucy killed her husband means nothing without the evidence of an affair. Add in the marks on her arms, and I'm thinking Steve will run with it."

I smiled. "That's all I want."

When he dropped me off at the Tiki Hut Grill, I went inside. Aunt Fern was not at the cash register, so I headed upstairs. I know Iggy would want to hear everything, as would Aunt Fern, but I decided it was my father who should be the one to tell his sister-in-law that he was some kind of animal shifter.

Since I'd had a long day, I decided to see if my aunt had figured out what to do about Bob Hatfield. That was a fairly safe topic, though it would take all of my control not to give her my two cents. I'd seen Penny try to make a bad situation work. And that failed. Seeing her with Hunter gave me hope that there was someone for everyone.

I knocked on her door.

"Come in," she called.

I entered. "Hey, Aunt Fern."

"Glinda. What's new?"

I told her about our visit to Carl Edwards' widow. "It's now in the hands of the sheriff."

"Once again, you and that handsome young man of yours solved the case."

I didn't want to tell her that Jaxson and I were not a couple—at least not yet. "Trust me. The sheriff would probably have figured it out eventually."

"I'm not so sure."

I loved how much she supported me. "I stopped over to see if you'd decided about what you were going to do with Bob."

"He and I had a long talk. While he promised not to bring up his deceased wife's name again, I didn't really believe him. I thanked him profusely for all the wonderful dinners, but I told him we weren't all that compatible."

"I'm sorry."

"For what? I was the one who decided he wasn't the one."

That would help her get over Bob faster. "What did Uncle Henry say?"

My aunt smiled. "I think he was both happy and sad. He knows he won't ever be replaced, so he is ready to cross over. I gave him my blessing."

"Does that mean he can't visit?" That would be kind of tragic.

"Knowing Henry, he'll find a way to come see me every now and again."

"I'm glad."

"Me too."

IT WAS AROUND four the next day when there was a knock at our office door, and I thought it was finally our first client. I jumped up and rushed over to welcome whoever was there. We really needed a sign that said to come in.

When I pulled open the door, who should be standing there but Steve and Nash. I didn't expect them. In fact, I was surprised they knew where we had our place of business. "Come in, gentlemen."

"Cozy," Steve said.

That was code for small. "Thank you. To what do I owe the honor?"

"May we sit?" Steve asked.

"Of course." They took up the sofa while I sat on a chair across from them. Jaxson was downstairs helping his brother. I could see that I would need some kind of signal to let him know when we had a visitor.

"Since I heard you convinced Mrs. Edwards to come forward with her husband's phone, we wanted to thank you."

My heart beat hard. "Does that mean you believe Lucy Owens killed Carl?"

"We do, and she did, but not solely based on the rather intimate messages between her and Carl. That just gave us a hint about her guilt."

I could see where this was going. "I'm guessing you decided to let Dr. Sanchez in on the world of the werewolf?"

Steve looked over at Nash. "Yes, but she has no idea who specifically can shift—just that some people can."

I did a zipping motion across my lips. "I won't tell a soul."

"Thank you. Anyway, Dr. Sanchez was able to compare the blood under the fingernails to that of Lucy's blood— blood we took from her scratch—and it was a match."

"She let you?" I asked.

"We had a warrant. When we showed the results to her, Lucy finally confessed that she killed Carl because of the way he treated her husband."

"That makes more sense."

We chatted a bit more about what was going to happen to her, as well as the general state of the clan. "Thank Jaxson, too. I know he had a big hand in solving this case."

I smiled. "He did." And so did Iggy.

"I know I should be telling you that it is wrong for you to insert yourself into so many of our cases, but I have to admit, your information has proven to be invaluable once more," Steve said.

Heat flushed my face at the unexpected compliment. "Thank you. I'm guessing you were able to prove that Carl killed Dirk?"

"Yes, we found the green bowling ball he used in the back of his closet. Not only that, the scoring mechanism never showed they played a game."

Just as I suggested. "I'm glad the case is closed. By the way, this weekend, I am hosting a small get together here to celebrate the opening of our new business, and I'd like you two to come."

"We'll be there. Thank you."

"Since I'm inviting all of the gossip queens, it might be in your best interest to make a connection with them."

Steve smiled. "I'm working on it."

"Oh, before you leave, I have a favor to ask." I held my breath, hoping he'd agree.

"I knew all of your information wasn't for free." Steve's smile told me he was kidding.

"Since my father doesn't have a ring like Nash's, I thought maybe he could borrow—"

"The garnet necklace that we keep in the bank's safety deposit box?" Steve asked.

"Yes. I know both necklaces belong to Emma Paxton, but I bet I could get her to agree to lend it to us. I don't want Dad to have it for longer than necessary. If those clan members ever found out, who knows what they would do," I said.

"I agree," Nash said. "That's why Hunter and I are working on a cure that we will only give to those we trust."

My knees weakened. "For real?"

"For real."

"Who will you ask to do the spell?"

"We aren't sure, but we'll find someone," Nash said.

As soon as they left, I raced down the back staircase to give Jaxson the news. He was on his computer. If I had to guess, he was ordering wine and maybe some cheese.

He looked up. "You seem happy."

"I am ecstatic."

Jaxson closed the lid. "Tell me."

I started with how Steve—using our information—was able to prove that Lucy Owens killed Carl Edwards, and I ended with Steve being willing to lend my father the garnet necklace for when the moon was full.

"You did it! If it weren't for you, Lucy would be a free woman," Jaxson said.

"You played an equal role."

He puffed out his chest. "I did, didn't I?" Then he laughed. "You do realize that once Iggy gets wind of all of this that he will be impossible to live with."

"He already is impossible to live with."

"I say this calls for a celebration to a job well done."

"I'm always up for celebrating. What do you have in mind?" I asked.

"I'd like to try that steak restaurant again in Hudson. This time we won't be so focused on avoiding Nash."

"That is a great idea. Doesn't it seem like a lifetime ago?"

"It does. And to add to the celebratory vibe, I, too, will be decked out in pink."

I laughed. The more time I spent with Jaxson Harrison, the more I liked him.

I HOPE you enjoyed seeing more of the townsfolk of Witch's Cove, and experiencing the life of her familiar, Iggy. Opening her own Pink Iguana Sleuth company with Jaxson Harrison certainly brought a whole new dimension to her life.

EXCERPT-NOT IN THE PINK

Don't forget to sign up for my Cozy Mystery newsletter *to learn about my discounts and upcoming releases. If you prefer to only receive notices regarding my releases, follow me on BookBub.*

Next up is Not in The Pink. Enjoy.

A pink iguana convinced he can talk to a cat ghost. A woman's psychic vision leading to another murder. And a witch who has no idea who to believe.

Hi, I'm Glinda Goodall, part-time witch and part-time amateur sleuth from Witch's Cove, Florida, a beach town full of witches and gossips.

Iggy--my talking pink iguana--just dropped a bomb on me, saying he just communicated with the ghost of some widow's pet. I might have dismissed that nonsense if the man didn't die the next day--just as this ghost cat had predicted! Now Iggy is determined to solve his murder, with or without my help.

I was losing faith that anyone would ever need my services as an amateur sleuth, when a high-profile woman shows up to our office claiming she had a vision of her husband being murdered and wants me to look into it. The problem? He's not dead. The sheriff dismissed her case, but that only gives me more reason to help her.

Things get really weird when her husband actually is murdered, and guess who's the number one suspect? You guessed it. This woman. There goes my first paying customer. I won't abandon her though. I'm determined to prove she's innocent.

When I'm not running around looking for clues, I waitress at the Tiki Hut Grill, so stop in for a smile and a great cup of coffee--or just to check in to see where I am in solving the case.

Here is Chapter 1

Hi, I'm Glinda Goodall, co-owner of The Pink Iguana Sleuths. We aren't doing any investigating right now since we can't seem to land any paying clients, but we are not giving up.

So, while we wait for someone to come knocking on our door, I've gone back to waitressing at my aunt's restaurant, the Tiki Hut Grill. Jaxson Harrison, my partner in this new business, has been earning a little extra cash loading wine for his brother who owns the Cheese and Wine Emporium located below our office.

Phew. That about sums up my life—well, almost. Now for the present.

After finishing a double shift at the restaurant, I was seriously in need of a solid eight hours of sleep. I dragged my tired body up the rear restaurant staircase and entered my apartment. Just as I was about to take off my pink bejeweled crown that was part of my waitress costume—as Glinda the Good Witch of the South, of course—my familiar, a pink iguana, jumped off his stool and charged.

I expected the little bugger to stop at my feet and do some

sort of excitement dance, but instead, he scrambled up my legs, shocking me when he grabbed my cheeks with his rather sharp claws and looked me in the eye.

Even though we'd been together fourteen years, he'd never done anything like that before. My surprise caused me to grab a hold of him with two hands and then hold him out at arm's length. "What in the world has gotten into you?"

"I saw a ghost! I saw a ghost!" His excitement had my own heart beating hard.

Okay, a normal person would either dismiss this as some kind of hallucination or be totally shocked at the existence of ghosts. Me? Neither was the case. You see, a few months ago, I too had seen and spoken to a ghost—or rather to two ghosts. And yes, my iguana can talk.

Before I continue about my familiar's newest revelation, I need to backtrack, because it will explain why it was reasonable to believe he could talk to a ghost. The reason Iggy ended up pink was because at the ripe old age of twelve, in the process of conjuring him, I messed up my spell. Shock, right? I often goofed up my spells.

Anyway, my theory was that since I only wore pink, my infatuation with the color must have caused him to change from green to pink. Being male, it embarrassed him, and I couldn't blame the poor little guy.

After years of him pestering me, I finally found a spell to change him back. The problem was that the witch who collected the ingredients became a bit preoccupied during the process and gave me one wrong ingredient. At the time, we were unaware of the glitch and drank the potion.

Instead of Iggy returning to his natural green state, we both ended up with the ability to see ghosts. Luckily for the first ghost we encountered, we were able to help him with the identity of the person who had murdered him.

Iggy wiggled in my hands. "Did you hear what I just said?" he asked not so nicely.

"You saw a ghost, did you? Was it Morgan Oliver again?" He was our first ghost.

"No. It was the ghost of a cat."

If I had been drinking tea, I might have spit it all over him. "A cat? Wow. I need a drink. Let's go into the kitchen, and you can tell me all about it."

Iggy had a lot of flaws, but out and out lying wasn't one of them. He did exaggerate—sometimes a lot—but he wouldn't make up something this important. I placed him on the two-person kitchen table and then grabbed a glass from the cabinet.

"While you were working—all day, I might add—I had nothing to do," Iggy said.

That was his usual ploy for sympathy. "Did you visit Aimee?"

Aimee was the black cat who lived across the hall with my aunt. Due to circumstances beyond Aimee's control, the same witch who messed up the potion that was supposed to return Iggy to green, accidentally gave Aimee the ability to speak. Iggy fancies himself her boyfriend, but too often she ignores him. And that causes him to be sad and sometimes rebellious.

"No, she wasn't home." For once, he didn't sound upset.

"What did you do instead?" I asked.

"I went outside. I hadn't even reached the beach board-walk when I felt a rush of cold air pass by me. Since I'd felt the same thing with Mr. Oliver—the ghost we helped—I figure he'd returned."

"That's logical, but the last time I communicated with him, he said he would be passing over now that he had no unfinished business."

"I remember. It turns out it wasn't Morgan Oliver. Before

I could figure out what was happening, this beautiful gray Persian cat blocks my way."

"Persian?"

"Yes. Her name is Sassy, but she wasn't nearly as transparent as Uncle Henry had been—or Morgan Oliver, for that matter. When I reached out to touch her, though, I felt nothing but air. It was creepy."

This was intriguing. I poured myself a glass of sweet iced tea and sat down at the kitchen table. "Was she able to communicate with you?"

"Yes, and here's the strange part. She isn't anyone's familiar."

"Then she couldn't talk." At least I was led to believe that only familiars had the power of speech—unless they were accidentally given the power, like Aimee had been.

"That's the thing. I'm an animal. She's an animal. While I can't talk to a random dog, I guess once an animal has crossed the rainbow bridge, they are given the power to communicate with familiars—at least that's my best guess."

"For real?"

"Of course, for real. How else would I know her name?"

I tossed back part of my drink. "Did Sassy say anything of interest?"

"Not at first. She was so thrilled to find someone who could hear her that she asked *me* a lot of questions."

"How long ago did she pass?"

Iggy tilted his head. "I don't know. Who cares? She's dead now."

I would have thought he'd have become a better detective than that by now. "Did you bother to find out whose pet she was?"

He scratched his face. I always thought it meant he was trying to recall a detail. "Yes. Before she *passed*, she belonged to Chester Hightower."

My heart went out to him. "He owns the Witch's Cove movie theater that I love."

My partner, Jaxson, had told me a few months back there was a rumor going around stating that someone wanted to buy the building, tear it down, and convert it into condos. While having a condo overlooking the Gulf of Mexico in sunny Florida would be wonderful for the occupants, it would be terrible for lovers of old movies. The memories I'd shared with friends at that theater had been immense.

"I know," Iggy said.

"I'm sorry to hear of his loss." Those words just tumbled out. That came as no surprise since my parents owned the Cove Funeral home.

"She said he was really sad about it."

"I can only imagine. Did she say anything else?"

"Yes. Sassy is really worried about Chester," Iggy said.

Sometimes Iggy could draw out a story way too long. "About what? Is his health failing?" The man had to be at least eighty.

"He thinks someone is trying to kill him."

I sucked in a breath. "No way. Does she know who?"

"No, but his theater is losing money, and his son, along with his deceased son's wife have been pressuring him to sell it to some big-time developer."

"I hope he doesn't give in. I know I'm often too tired to go to the movies, but when I do, the classics move me."

"Apparently, not enough people feel the same way."

"Now you're an expert?" That snarky comment wasn't called for, but hearing that Chester Hightower was having troubles upset me.

"No worse than you." He turned his snout toward me, which meant he wasn't looking at me since his eyes were on the side of his head. That was his passive aggressive stance.

"Make me feel bad, why don't you? Maybe you can ask

Sassy to return to her old haunt and find out who wants him dead."

"I suggested that, but she said being back home might creep her out."

"Seriously? I didn't know cats cared enough." To be honest, I knew very little about cats and their feelings.

"I did ask her who she thought wanted him dead."

"And?" I asked.

"She didn't know for sure, but she doesn't trust either the widowed daughter-in-law or his son, Darren."

"Really? Darren Hightower, who runs the theater, is a nice guy. According to several knowledgeable people, he's donated his time and money to many good causes."

"He might be a saint, but that doesn't mean he didn't urge old dad to sell. That property would bring the family a lot of money, I bet."

"You're right. I remember when Darren's brother died three years ago. The rumor mill claimed he didn't leave his wife, Amanda, with a ton of money."

"See? Both Mr. Hightower's daughter-in-law and son have a motive to want the old guy dead," Iggy said. "As for me? I just want to help Sassy."

His interest seemed to be more than a desire to help. "Do you like this ghost cat or something?"

"She's pretty, for sure."

"Iggy Goodall. You have a girlfriend. What about Aimee?"

"What about her?"

I wasn't sure how to answer. Clearly, I had failed to raise him responsibly. "Fidelity is one of the most important components in a relationship."

He lifted his chest. "I'm trying to be a good person. Don't worry. I am fully aware that Sassy is dead, which means it's not like I can actually have any physical contact with her. I'm betting I never see her again. I think she only appeared to ask me to help find the person who was after Mr. Hightower."

Iggy really seemed to want to help. "How about if I speak with him? I'll ask Jaxson to do a little digging into who wants to buy the theater and for how much. I'm betting Mr. Hightower himself has an idea who might be targeting him."

Iggy jumped up and down. "Yes, thank you." He scurried off the table and ran out of the kitchen.

"Where are you going?"

"To tell Sassy the good news."

I jumped up from the table and dashed after him. "You said you didn't know how to contact her."

"I never said that." With that, my precious iguana was out the cat door.

I suppose that since ghosts don't sleep, she might be hanging about. As for me? I needed to go to bed. Tomorrow, I wasn't working at the restaurant, which would give me time to discuss our new pro bono case with Jaxson and see how he wanted to handle it.

Since Iggy could take care of himself, I headed to my bedroom, despite my mind spinning. I know one thing I could do to help—put a protection spell around Mr. Hightower to keep away the evil until Jaxson and I could figure out who wanted the man dead.

The End

ABOUT THE AUTHOR

Love it HOT and STEAMY? Sign up for my newsletter and receive MONTANA DESIRE for FREE. Click here

OR Are you a fan of quirky PARANORMAL COZY MYSTERIES? Sign up for this newsletter. Click Here

Not only do I love to read, write, and dream, I'm an extrovert. I enjoy being around people and am always trying to understand what makes them tick. Not only must my romance books have a happily ever after, I need characters I can relate to. My men are wonderful, dynamic, smart, strong, and the best lovers in the world (of course).

My Paranormal Cozy Mysteries are where I let my imagination run wild with witches and a talking pink iguana who believes he's a real sleuth.

I believe I am the luckiest woman. I do what I love and I have a wonderful, supportive husband, who happens to be hot!

Fun facts about me
(1) I'm a math nerd who loves spreadsheets. Give me numbers and I'll find a pattern.
(2) I live on a Costa Rica beach!
(3) I also like to exercise. Yes, I know I'm odd.

I love hearing from readers either on FB or via email (hint, hint).

Social Media Sites

Website: www.velladay.com
FB: www.facebook.com/vella.day.90
Twitter: velladay4
Gmail: velladayauthor@gmail.com
Tiktok: Velladayauthor1
Bookbub: https://www.bookbub.com/authors/vella-day

ALSO BY VELLA DAY

Ghosts and PINK Candles (book 14)

Pilfered PINK Pearls (book 15)

Box Set (books 13-15)

The Case of the Stolen PINK Tombstone (book 16)

The PINK Christmas Cookie Caper (book 17)

PINK Moon Rising (book 18)

Box set(books 16-18)

The PINK Wedding Dress Whodunit (book 19)

SILVER LAKE SERIES (3 OF THEM)

A TASTE OF SILVER LAKE

Weres and Witches Box Set (books 1-2)

Hidden Realms Box Set (books 1-2)

Goddesses of Destiny Box Set (books 1-2)

(1). **HIDDEN REALMS OF SILVER LAKE** (Paranormal Romance)

Awakened By Flames (book 1)

Seduced By Flames (book 2)

Box Set (books 1-2)

Kissed By Flames (book 3)

Destiny In Flames (book 4)

Box Set (books 3-4)

Passionate Flames (book 5)

Ignited By Flames (book 6)

Box Set (books 5-6)

Touched By Flames (book 7)

Bound By Flames (book 8)

Box set (books 7-8)

Fueled By Flames (book 9)

Scorched By Flames (book 10)

Box Set (books 9-10)

(2). **GODDESSES OF DESTINY** Paranormal Romance)

Slade (book 1)

Rafe (book 2)

Will (book 3)

Josh (book 4)

Jace (book 5)

Tanner (book 6)

(3). **WERES AND WITCHES OF SILVER LAKE** (Paranormal Romance)

A Magical Shift (book 1)

Catching Her Bear (book 2)

Surge of Magic (book 3)

The Bear's Forbidden Wolf (book 4)

Box Set (books 1-4)

Her Reluctant Bear (book 5)

Freeing His Tiger (book 6)

Protecting His Wolf (book 7)

Waking His Bear (book 8)

Box Set (books 5-8)

Melting Her Wolf's Heart (book 9)

Her Wolf's Guarded Heart (book 10)

His Rogue Bear (book 11)

Reawakening Their Bears (book 12)

Box Set (books 9-12)

OTHER PARANORMAL SERIES

PACK WARS (Paranormal Romance)

Training Their Mate (book 1)

Claiming Their Mate (book 2)

Rescuing Their Virgin Mate (book 3)

Box Set (books 1-3)

Loving Their Vixen Mate (book 4)

Fighting For Their Mate (book 5)

Enticing Their Mate (book 6)

Box Set (books 4-6)

Their Huntress Mate (book 7)

Craving Their Mate (book 8)

PACK WARS-THE GRANGERS

Meant for them (book 1)

Meant for wolves (book 2)

Meant for forever (book 3)

Meant for her (book 4)

Meant for two (book 5)

HIDDEN HILLS SHIFTERS (Paranormal Romance)

An Unexpected Diversion (book 1)

Bare Instincts (book 2)

Shifting Destinies (book 3)

Embracing Fate (book 4)

Promises Unbroken (book 5)

Bare 'N Dirty (book 6)

Hidden Hills Shifters Complete Box Set (books 1-6)

CONTEMPORARY SERIES

MONTANA PROMISES (Full length contemporary Romance)

Promises of Mercy (book 1)

Foundations For Three (book 2)

Montana Fire (book 3)

Montana Promises Box Set (books 1-3)

Hart To Hart (Book 4)

Burning Seduction (Book 5)

Montana Promises Complete Box Set (books 1-5)

Novellas:

Montana Desire (book 1)

Awakening Passions (book 2)

PLEDGED TO PROTECT (contemporary romantic suspense)

From Panic To Passion (book 1)

From Danger To Desire (book 2)

From Terror To Temptation (book 3)

BURIED SERIES (contemporary romantic suspense)

Buried Alive (book 1)

Buried Secrets (book 2)

Buried Deep (book 3)

The Buried Series Complete Box Set (books 1-3)

A NASH MYSTERY (Contemporary Romance)

Sidearms and Silk(book 1)

Black Ops and Lingerie(book 2)

A Nash Mystery Box Set (books 1-2)

STARTER SETS (Romance)

<u>Contemporary</u>

<u>Paranormal</u>